THE
SILENT
SPEAK

VAL COLLINS

The main character in this book is Aoife. This is a very common Irish name and is pronounced "Eee-fah".

A minor character is called Triona (Thre-ona). This is an abbreviation of Caitriona (Catherine)

Two characters who are mentioned occasionally are Bronagh (Bro-nah) and Caoimhe (Kwee-vah)

All are common Irish names. If you would like to hear the names pronounced, check out my Instagram post here: *https://bit.ly/3npIiEQ*

If you are interested in my previous thrillers, GIRL TARGETED and ONLY LIES REMAIN, you can check them out on my website here: *http://bit.ly/2Xw7vTb*

PROLOGUE

SHE READ THE note again.

Twice in the past three years, similar notes had been splashed all over the newspapers. She knew immediately what it meant, but her brain wouldn't allow her to process it. For several minutes she just stared at it. Her lips formed words that never came. When her brain caught up, it went straight to denial.

This could not be happening.

Things like this did not happen in ordinary families.

Not in families like hers.

She pulled down the door handle. The door was unlocked. That was a good sign, right? She would go into the house and find everything exactly as it had always been. There just had to be some simple explanation for that note. Yes, she nodded to herself, relieved to have come to a decision. She nudged the door open and put one foot on the wooden floor. The house was eerily quiet. No kids running around. No noise from the kitchen.

'Now don't panic,' she muttered to herself. 'Everything will be fine. Just go inside.'

She tried to lift her foot, but her brain wouldn't cooperate. Hands shaking, she pulled out her mobile and dialled 999. She was still frozen in the doorway when the police arrived.

ONE

IT TOOK AOIFE a few seconds to realise Conor wasn't listening. His eyes were focused on a point behind her head, and his face had taken on that wooden expression, the only expression he had shown her in the first few months of their acquaintance.

'Is something wrong?'

Conor didn't appear to hear. He pushed back his chair and walked away. Aoife glanced behind. She saw a woman hurry towards him. They met in the centre of the room. The woman wore jeans and a rain jacket. She had shoulder-length chocolate-brown hair, pulled back into a tight ponytail. She was a little older than Conor, probably in her mid-thirties. Not stunningly pretty by any means, but good looking. She was gesticulating wildly as she spoke. Conor answered her in a low voice. For the sake of appearances, Aoife picked at her food, but she concentrated hard, trying to catch their words above the noise of the crowd.

Conor's voice was a low hum, but she clearly heard the woman say 'not answering my calls' and 'what do I have to do to get…'

Abandoning any pretence at politeness, Aoife turned in her chair and stared. Conor now had his hand on the woman's arm and was leading her towards the exit. She jerked her arm away. Her eyes met Aoife's. She said something which Aoife didn't catch and tried to push past Conor. Conor's hand was on her arm again, but this time his grip was tighter. The woman tried to yank her arm away but was unable to get free. There was a lull in the conversation as people watched the drama. The restaurant manager approached. He and Conor exchanged a few words. The manager took the woman's other arm and they led her to the door. The woman struggled but couldn't escape. As the manager went to close the door behind her, she turned to face them. Again, her eyes met Aoife's. She was crying.

The drama over, the other diners resumed their conversations. Conor returned to his seat.

'What was that about?' Aoife asked. 'Who is that woman?'

'Nobody, it's work.'

'Work? Why is she so upset?'

'I'd rather not talk about it, Aoife. It's our last weekend before Blaine arrives. We won't have time alone again for weeks. Why waste it talking about work?'

Aoife felt her stomach sink—its normal reaction to any

mention of Blaine's visit. 'Do you want me to come to the airport with you?'

'No, I think it's best I go alone. I'll bring him home. Let him unpack and settle in and then we'll come around to your house. He's looking forward to seeing Amy again.'

Aoife smiled. 'I'm glad those two hit it off. If only—'

Conor put down his glass and leaned closer. 'I've told you, Aoife, Blaine doesn't hate you.'

'How often has he been in my house now, Conor? In all that time the only words he's said to me are "hi", "bye", "please", "thank you", "yes" and "no". That's it.'

'It's not easy for him. He's used to having me entirely to himself.'

'I get that, Conor. I do, really. I understand there's nothing in our relationship for him. That's what makes it harder. I have nothing at all to offer him.' She squashed a couple of peas with her fork. Unable to make eye contact, she said, 'Maybe it would be better if he spent less time in my house.'

When Conor didn't reply, she looked at him. 'Spend the week together and come for dinner at the weekend. If Blaine has more time with you, he might be less resentful of me.'

Conor gave her suggestion a moment's consideration, then shook his head. 'I don't think that would be a good idea. You, I and Amy are going to be a family. I don't want Blaine to feel like an outsider. He needs to spend time with us in order to fit into our new family. Katie says it took him almost a year to accept his stepfather. He just needs time to get used to you.'

'Wasn't he six when Katie got married? Fifteen is a whole different ballgame. Don't damage your relationship with Blaine by trying to force him to like me. You only have him to yourself a few times a year as it is. In three years he'll be in college and you'll see him even less. Enjoy the time together and forget about me. When he's in college it won't matter as much that you have a life of your own.'

Conor ran his fingers through his hair. The product he'd used that morning was wearing off and it was threatening to turn curly again. 'It would certainly be easier, and I know he'd enjoy his visits more.' He picked up his fork but immediately put it down again. 'The problem is, Aoife, I don't want to have a life of my own. I want Blaine to be a part of my new life.'

'I know, honey, but I don't think that can happen until he's older. If Blaine lived in Ireland, then obviously we'd have to try, but on his few visits here, why force him to do something he hates?'

Conor sighed. 'How about this? We'll spend the first night in my house and I'll bring him around on Saturday afternoon. After that, we'll have every day together but we'll come to your house for dinner each evening. That way he'll get some time with me and some time with you and Amy. We might even bring Amy on the odd day trip if we're not going too far.' He smiled. 'Actually, Blaine's looking forward to seeing Amy again. Katie helped him pick out a present and he's excited to give it to her.'

'Okay, but Blaine loves you. I think he even loves Amy. If he doesn't want to be around me, what does it matter?'

'It matters to me, but maybe I shouldn't push it.' Conor cut a piece of meat, swallowed, then grinned at her. 'And maybe we should stop worrying about Blaine for a while and enjoy our last weekend together. You, Aoife Walsh, are the love of my life, and the sooner you agree to be my wife—'

Aoife leaned across the table and kissed him. It wasn't something she would normally do in a crowded restaurant, but she was desperate to change the subject. Hell, she would do almost anything to postpone another argument about her refusal to become officially engaged.

TWO

FOUR DAYS LATER, on the dot of noon, Aoife was sitting in the basement of Fallon & Byrne. She sipped her coffee as she read her book. Her phone had been buzzing every few minutes for the last two weeks as the members of her book club discussed *The Handmaid's Tale*. Aoife had only opened it that morning. She was midway through page seventy-two when she heard the clicking of heels on the stairs. She knew it was Orla even before the highly polished Christian Louboutin shoes came into view. The hem of her royal blue dress was so sharply cut it could only be the product of a top designer. As more of Orla appeared, Aoife noticed her customary blonde curls had been tamed into a smooth bun. Orla had always dressed for the part. As a teenager, she could have walked straight off the set of *The O.C.* She was a fashionable but casually dressed college student, and now she looked every inch the successful barrister she intended to become. She strode across the tiled floor, almost bumping into a woman heading in the same direction.

Orla gave her a gracious smile. 'Excuse me.'

The woman blushed, turned around and scurried off to a table in the corner of the room. Orla pulled out the chair opposite Aoife and sank into it.

'I'm sorry I'm late, Aoife. I had a nightmare meeting with a client. Honestly, you don't want to know the morning I've had. Anyway, thank God, I'm finished for today. I've taken the entire afternoon off and we can hit the shops the minute I've had a cup of coffee.' She smiled. 'How was your weekend?'

'Great. Conor brought up the whole engagement thing again, which was a bit awkward, but fortunately he let it drop.'

'You can't keep avoiding the subject forever, Aoife. Conor knows your divorce won't come through for a while. All he's asking for is a commitment.'

'You know I'm committed to Conor. And if Conor doesn't know that by now, I'm not sure what we're doing together. Orla, do we have to talk about this? I'm sick to death of the subject.'

'Okay.' Orla raised her hands in a gesture of defeat. 'I won't mention it again.' She glanced at the book sticking out of Aoife's bag. 'How's that book club of yours?'

'Not great. When Jenny talked me into joining, I was worried they met too often, but lately it feels more like an online book club. The WhatsApp group is very active but we've only met twice since I joined. Ruth seems to have lost interest in organising it, and everyone else is afraid to take on the role in case they upset her.'

'Because of the murder? That must have been a huge shock to all of you. I think the whole country was shocked. It was all over the paper for weeks. That Grogan guy must have been a real nutter. You'd have to be pretty crazy to kill your wife and kids like that. Were Ruth and Fiona close?'

'I don't know. I barely know Ruth. Jenny says she used to be brilliant at organising everybody and she kept the WhatsApp group going but the only sessions she attended regularly were the ones she hosted herself. You really should come at least once, Orla. You'd love it and you'd finally get a chance to meet...'

'What?'

'That woman you almost bumped into; she keeps staring at us.'

'Really!' Orla turned to look. 'She's probably a weirdo. They seem to be crawling out of the woodwork lately. Did I tell you about the woman who came up to me in Brown Thomas last week? She said if I had to flirt with her husband, could I at least have the decency to do it behind her back. Brown Thomas! Can you imagine! If you're not safe from the riff-raff in Brown Thomas, where are you safe?'

'You were flirting with her husband?'

'Of course not. Why on earth would I want to do that?'

'She just decided you were flirting for no reason?'

'Since I have no idea who her husband is, I can't think of any other explanation.'

'So, what happened?'

'I said, "I have no idea what you're talking about, but assuming you are around the same age as your husband, he's old enough to be my father. Do I look like the kind of girl who flirts with middle-aged—"'

'Oh look, she's leaving!' Aoife interrupted. The woman gathered up her belongings and almost ran up the stairs. 'She looks vaguely familiar. Should we know her?'

Orla glanced at the retreating back. 'I don't see how. She must be at least ten years older than us, so she couldn't know us from school, and it's unlikely we were in college together.' She took a small silver compact from her Chanel bag and examined her flawless make-up. 'Just another weirdo if you ask me.' Clicking the compact shut, she said, 'Now, are you sure you want to buy a new outfit, Aoife? Exactly how formal is Conor's function?'

'It's not black tie, but all the women dress up.'

'It's a good thing I spent half of Saturday in Brown Thomas, then. I bought four outfits. One's a bit casual, but any of the others would be perfect and they'd all look stunning on you.'

THREE

'BLAINEY!' AMY TURNED from the window where she had been keeping watch for the last twenty minutes. Her eyes blazing with excitement, she shouted, 'Blainey! Blainey!' and raced out to the hall. Aoife heard Conor's key in the door, Amy's excited prattle and Conor's laugh. She took a moment to gather herself, then went out to greet them. Amy was in Blaine's arms. He threw her into the air and she screamed with delight. He had grown several inches since Christmas and already towered over Aoife. He'd soon be as tall as his father.

'Hi, Blaine,' she said.

It was as if a light switch had been flicked off. The entire hallway seemed to darken. Blaine put Amy on the floor. His whole body tensed as he turned to face her.

'Hi,' he said.

She caught her breath. Those eyes! They always came as a shock when she hadn't seen him for a while. At first glance

Blaine and Conor looked nothing alike. Blaine was at the tall, gangly stage, although he would probably fill out like his father. They both had pale complexions, but Blaine's hair was blond and straight while Conor's was dark and so curly he never went to work without slicking it down. 'Have you ever seen a detective with a head of boyish curls?' he said when Aoife laughed at him. The one thing Blaine and Conor shared was their intense deep blue eyes. But whereas Conor's eyes lit up every time he looked at Aoife, Blaine's had a slightly wary expression.

'Blainey bought me a present.' Amy scowled. 'But he won't give it to me. Moaney, make him give me my present.'

'Conor,' Aoife said.

Conor smiled. 'Moaney is fine and Blaine's teasing you, Amy. Your present is in the car.'

Amy tugged at Blaine's arm. 'I want my present now, Blainey!'

'Ask nicely, Amy.'

'Please can I have my present, Blainey? Please! Please!'

Blaine grinned at her. 'Okay.'

Amy raced out to the car and Blaine followed.

'Do you really not mind her calling you Moaney?' Aoife asked.

'I like it. She's the only person in the world that calls me that. It makes it special.' He put his arm around Aoife and pulled her close. 'Relax. It's all going to be fine. Just give it time.'

A few minutes later, Amy came running into the

hall, waving a doll in the air. 'Super Girl! Blainey got me Super Girl!'

'Did you say thank you?'

'Thank you, Blainey.' She gave him a quick hug. 'I'm going to show Carly.' She ran through the kitchen and out the back door. Climbing up on the swing, she shouted, 'Carly! Carly!'

'Amy! Don't stand on the swing!'

'I'll get her.' Conor went into the garden, hoisted Amy on his shoulders and carried her over to the wall that separated her house from that of her best friend. Aoife could see her waving her doll in the air and heard Carly's excited squeals.

'That was a lovely present, Blaine. Thank you.'

'It's okay.' He looked at the ground. 'I'll er… er…' He shrugged and went out into the garden. The minute he escaped, his entire personality seemed to change. He climbed up onto the wall and jumped into the next-door neighbour's garden. A few seconds later the top of his head appeared over the wall. He was carrying Carly on his shoulders. Blaine began dancing the length of the wall and Conor copied him. The two little girls shrieked with laughter as they tried to touch hands across the wall. Conor had his head thrown back and she could hear Blaine's laughter. Aoife's eyes filled with tears. She felt like an outsider in her own home. She knew if she joined them, the atmosphere would turn to ice in a second.

FOUR

Lisa

WHEN THEY LEFT, Lisa put her arms around her mother. 'Ignore them. They can't force us to do anything.'

Her mother's hands shook as she reached for a tissue. 'They've been through enough. If this will help them cope, I'll have to agree.'

'You don't have to agree to anything, Mum. Shane is with his family, where he belongs. They have no right to even suggest such a horrific thing. What about us? Aren't we allowed to have any feelings?'

'Maybe you are. I'm not. They think this is all my fault.'

The pain in her eyes was so stark, Lisa had to turn away. She took a deep breath and forced herself to meet her mother's gaze.

'That's ridiculous, Mum. How could any of this be your fault?'

'I raised him.'

'You raised a kind, thoughtful, loving man. Whatever anyone else might say, you and I know the truth. Don't listen to them. Don't listen to anyone.'

'Fiona was their daughter, and those beautiful babies…' She brought the tissue to her eyes to hide her tears.

Lisa kissed the top of her mother's head. 'This has got to stop. We've all been hurt enough. They have no right to make things worse. We are not going to allow them to separate Shane from his family.'

Her mother pushed back her chair and stood up. 'I'll allow it. It's the very least I can do.'

'Mum!'

Her mother shuffled towards the door. 'I'm going to lie down for a bit. Please don't mention the subject again, Lisa. I've made up my mind. If this is what they need to heal, this is how it's going to be.'

Lisa sat on the sofa. She bit her lip, tears spilling onto her cheeks. Her tears turned to sobs and within a few minutes she had to bury her head in a cushion to drown out the howls of anguish.

FIVE

IT HAD BEEN a hell of a day in the office. Aoife's computer had crashed and she'd lost hours of work. Normally she finished at noon on Wednesdays, but she had to stay in the office until 2 p.m. to redo the work she'd lost. As if that wasn't bad enough, a crash on the motorway meant her normally fifteen-minute commute took almost an hour. The only music to hand was children's nursery rhymes, so Aoife switched on the radio. For a full twenty minutes she channel-hopped between the most boring programmes ever broadcast, finally settling on an interview with a well-known politician. His views were so contrary to her own that she screamed at the radio in protest. When Aoife finally pulled into her driveway, exhausted and irritated, her humour was not improved by the sight of Jason's car in her driveway. That was all she needed! What was he doing here? He saw Amy every second weekend. Never once had he suggested seeing her during the week.

Aoife let herself into the house. Somewhere in the distance she could hear a kids' movie. Jason and Blaine were sitting at the kitchen table deep in conversation, an empty pizza box on the table between them.

'Hi, Aoife.'

'Jason, what are you doing here? Where's Conor?'

'He was called into work urgently. He rang Mum to see if she could take Amy, but I was there, so I came around.'

'Why didn't you bring Amy back to your own place or to Maura's?'

'Mum's having the entire house repainted. She spent last night with me because the fumes were so bad. It's better now but I don't know if it would be safe for Amy. In any case, Amy didn't want to leave Blaine, and he wasn't too keen on meeting his father's girlfriend's ex-mother-in-law-to-be.' He glanced at Blaine and they both laughed. Aoife felt her anger soar.

'Right, where's Amy?'

'She got bored hanging out with us adults. She went upstairs to watch some movie.'

So rather than spend time with his daughter, he was letting Disney do the babysitting again. And why had he put a slight emphasis on 'adults'? Was he trying to flatter Blaine?

'Jason, I would prefer if you did not allow Amy to watch TV during the day.'

'Relax, Aoife. A little TV won't do her any harm.' Again, he glanced at Blaine. Blaine's lips twitched.

Aoife marched out to the corridor. 'Amy! Come say goodbye to your dad.'

Amy came running down the stairs.

'Bye, Daddy.' She gave him a hug.

Jason stood. 'I guess I'm leaving. It was nice meeting you, Blaine. I hope you enjoy your holiday.'

As soon as the car was out of the driveway, Amy ran upstairs to her movie. Aoife followed her. 'Give me the iPad, Amy, please. You are not allowed to watch TV during the day.'

'Daddy said I could.'

'You do what Daddy says in Daddy's house. You do what I say in this house.'

Amy scowled. She gripped the iPad with both hands and held it against her tiny body. 'You're a very mean mummy.'

'Amy!'

'Amy, would you like me to push you on the swing?' Aoife hadn't heard Blaine coming up the stairs.

'Yes, please.' Her temper tantrum forgotten, Amy flung the iPad on the bed and ran down the stairs. A few minutes later, Aoife heard the squeak of the swing and intermittent peals of laughter. She switched off the iPad, sat on Amy's bed and buried her head in her hands.

'I'm sorry. I thought he was coming around to collect Amy. I didn't realise he was going to spend the entire afternoon in the house.'

'I was so furious. And it made me even madder that he and Blaine seem to have become great friends.'

'I know.' Conor came up behind her, wrapped his arms around her and kissed her neck. 'They don't often call me in when I'm on holidays, but if it happens again, I'll bring her to Maura's myself or I'll drop her into your office.'

'Dad, when are we leaving? I told Mum I'd phone her tonight.'

Conor kept an arm around Aoife's waist as he turned to face his son. 'We're having dinner here, Blaine. I thought you knew that.'

'Again!'

'Blaine!'

'Sorry, it's just that I wanted to talk to Mum.'

'If you need privacy, phone her from the car.'

'Amy will follow me.'

Aoife pulled away from Conor. 'I'll make sure she doesn't bother you, Blaine. Dinner will be in twenty minutes.'

Running down the stairs, Aoife realised she couldn't smell the chicken. She felt the oven door. Cold. The chicken inside was warm. 'Damn!'

'What's wrong, honey?' Conor and Blaine had followed her downstairs.

'Dinner is ruined. Amy, did you turn off the oven?'

Amy was sitting at the kitchen table, colouring.

'No,' she said, her tongue hanging out as she concentrated on her task.

Aoife could tell she wasn't lying. 'How did it get turned off? The chicken is warm, so the oven must have been hot when I put it in.'

'Maybe you turned it off by accident?'

'Why would I do that, Conor? Well, we can't eat it now. We could all get food poisoning. How do you feel about omelettes?'

'Great. I'll make the salad. You love omelettes, don't you, Blaine?'

'I don't mind.'

Aoife looked at him. Had she imagined the note of triumph in his voice? She glanced at Conor, but he didn't appear to have noticed.

Aoife and Amy were waving goodbye as Conor and Blaine drove away. Amy always ran to the gate, waving frantically, but this time she followed them out to the road. Aoife's house was on the edge of the Curragh. A narrow road separated it from miles and miles of flat planes which were occupied mostly by sheep, their lambs and the occasional horse. When she and Jason had moved in, the road had been an uneven path with enormous potholes and very little traffic. Last year it had been properly surfaced. It still didn't get much traffic, but the few cars that used the road tended to drive at ridiculous speeds. Aoife called her back, but Amy ignored her. Aoife listened. No traffic. She hurried inside, grabbed her house keys and ran after Amy. From the gate, she could see Amy a little way in the distance talking to a woman. It was quite common for locals to walk through the fields, but they rarely walked on the road.

'Amy!'

Amy ran towards her and the woman followed. 'This is my mummy.'

Aoife picked Amy up. The woman held out her hand. 'Hi, I'm Lisa.'

Aoife recognised her immediately.

'Hi.'

'Do you remember me?'

'You were in Fallon & Byrne.'

'Yes. I was going to speak to you, but your friend arrived before I had a chance. That was the second time we met. I also saw you in the restaurant with Detective Moloney.'

'That was you?' Aoife looked at her warily. Amy was wriggling in her arms. Aoife put her on the ground, and she ran towards a group of young lambs who appeared to be trying to climb a tree. They fled in terror and she raced across the field after them. 'Stay where I can see you, Amy,' Aoife called. She turned to the woman.

'How do you know where I live?'

'I've been following Detective Moloney.'

Aoife took a step backwards and glanced towards Amy.

'I'm not a stalker. I'm Shane Grogan's sister.'

'Shane? Fiona's husband?'

'You knew Fiona?'

'No. We never actually met, but she was in my book club. My friend Jenny knew her.'

'Oh yeah, I remember Fiona mentioning something

about them joining a book club. It's hard to believe there was a time when finding a book club that would take her was one of her biggest problems.'

'I'm so sorry about what happened. I can't even imagine what you're going through.'

'Most of the time I'm not too sure myself. It's been four months already and I still can't really believe it happened.'

'Did you want to discuss the murder with Conor?'

'I wish I could. I've been trying to talk to him for months. You know he's the lead detective in the investigation?'

Aoife shook her head. 'Conor doesn't discuss his work with me.'

Lisa snorted. 'He doesn't discuss it with me either, and Shane was my family. That night in the restaurant he had me thrown out. I thought you would be more likely to listen to me.'

'I think Conor was upset you approached him outside the office. His son is visiting, so he's taken a few weeks off work, but I'm sure the office can let you know who's taken over his cases.'

'I've spoken to his replacement. He's worse than Detective Moloney. No matter what I say, the answer I get is "I understand". I don't want his understanding, I want him to find the killer. You have to help me. I'm desperate.'

'Lisa, I truly am sorry for your loss, but I don't see what I can do to help.'

'I need—I'm sorry, I don't know your name.'

'Aoife.'

'Aoife, I need you to convince Detective Moloney that my brother is not a murderer.'

'How can I do that? I never even met Shane.'

'My brother wasn't capable of murdering anyone, let alone his own family. His youngest was a little younger than your daughter. What kind of a monster would murder a two-year-old? There's a lunatic out there who butchered five innocent people and nobody is looking for him. Please, you have to convince Detective Moloney to listen to me.'

Aoife nodded towards Amy, who was now halfway across the field. 'I have to get her.'

She walked away, but Lisa followed. 'Think how you would feel if you were me. Fiona's family say they were in shock when they agreed to have Shane buried with his wife and kids. They want his grave dug up and his remains moved to another cemetery. My mother is seventy-two. She's barely survived the last four months. This will kill her. Please help me.'

'We have to go home now, Amy.' Aoife reached for her hand and Amy skipped along beside her. Lisa followed them back to the house.

'You're my only hope,' Lisa said. 'There's nobody else I can turn to.'

'Why is that lady crying, Mummy?'

Aoife opened the front door and Amy ran inside. 'I'm sorry, I have to go.'

'But you'll talk to Detective Moloney? Just get him to sit down with me. That's all I'm asking.'

'I'll think about it.'

SIX

Lisa

LISA TURNED THE key in the ignition but made no attempt to move. Had she been convincing enough? If Aoife didn't help her, what would she do? Her heart was thumping in her chest, she was finding it difficult to catch her breath, and her vision blurred. She checked her pulse. It was racing so fast she couldn't get a count. Did women in their thirties have heart attacks? She needed to get a bit of perspective. If Aoife wouldn't help them, it wasn't the end of the world. So Shane would be separated from his family, it wasn't like any of them would know what was going on, was it? But that wasn't the way her mother would see it. Lisa knew the thought of Shane's body being dug up was draining what remained of her mother's once-indomitable spirit. It was killing her that the entire country assumed her son was a monster. And not just any monster, a monster who could cut the throats of his own children. Knowing that other suspects were being considered would give her mother some relief. Lisa leaned back against the headrest and shut her eyes. She concentrated on controlling her breathing. Her pulse slowed, then returned to normal, but Lisa kept her eyes shut and tried to appreciate the solitude. She was so tired. If only she could go home to a place of her own, lock the door and not speak to another person for at least a year, she might be able to cope. Not happy with that image, she pictured herself breaking the speed limit the entire way to the airport and hopping on a last-minute flight to Australia or New Zealand. She would find a house overlooking the beach and forget she'd ever lived any other life. She let her mind wander to images of herself lying on the sand with the burning sun beating down on her. All the muscles in her body relaxed, and her lips formed into a tiny smile. Then the scene changed abruptly to one of her mother sitting alone in a dark room with nobody to comfort her. Lisa took a deep breath, fastened her seat belt and drove home.

SEVEN

'YOU SPOKE TO Shane Grogan's sister? When? Where?'

'She followed you to my house. When you left, Amy ran after the car. By the time I caught up with her, she was talking to Lisa.'

Conor reached for his phone. 'That's it. Phoning me two, three times a day, I can cope with, but first the restaurant and now this? I've tried to be patient with her, but she's gone too far.'

Aoife put her hand on his arm. 'Conor, please don't.'

'I can't have her following us. The woman is unhinged. I know that's probably not her fault. I'd be unhinged if I found my family butchered, but—'

'She's not unhinged. She's just upset. Who wouldn't be in the circumstances? She says the police won't talk to her. All she wants is for you to sit down and listen to what she has to say.'

'I know what she has to say. I must have listened to it

ten thousand times by now. She doesn't believe her brother murdered his family. But all the evidence says he did.'

'What evidence?'

'I don't want to talk about it, Aoife. I won't bring my work home to you and Amy.'

'Well, certainly not to Amy, but I'd like you to speak to me about your work. It's a big part of your life and I want to be involved.'

Conor shook his head. 'You really don't. I wish I'd never heard of the damn case. I don't even like to think about it when I'm not on duty and I certainly don't want to be responsible for you thinking about it. I'll never forget that crime scene. Those poor little kids! The one person they should have been able to trust and he butchered them. Do you know the eldest tried to protect his little sister? He was only nine.'

Aoife wrapped her arms around Conor's waist and rested her head against his back. When his body began to relax, she pulled away to look at him. 'Lisa says her brother wasn't capable of hurting anyone.'

'I know. She's told me that at least once a day for the last four months.'

'But you believe he's a murderer?'

Conor sighed. 'You read about the note in the papers. "Don't come in. Call the police. I'm sorry." What other explanation could there be for pinning that note to the front door?'

'Isn't that the same note that O'Leary guy left on his front door after he killed his family?'

'Almost word for word.'

'Could it be a copycat thing? Somebody wanted to murder the family, so they copied the O'Leary case?'

'It was Shane Grogan's handwriting. I had it analysed. Of course, Lisa won't accept it. I can understand it's difficult for her. Everyone who knew the family was shocked. Grogan appeared to be a pleasant, kind man. Everyone says he and his wife seemed happy and the kids were well adjusted, but some people just snap without any warning. When Grogan realised what he'd done, he put that note on the door and killed himself. It's happened before all over the world. It's happened here twice in the past three years. Shane Grogan was the third.'

'You're absolutely sure nobody else was involved?'

'We've gone over all the evidence, Aoife. We've taken fingerprints and DNA samples. There's no reason to suspect any outside involvement.'

'You could account for all the DNA and every single fingerprint?'

'No, of course not. They were a sociable house. The kids' friends were in and out every day. All the neighbours had been invited for drinks on New Year's Eve, and they'd had a fortieth birthday party less than a month before the murder. There were fingerprints and DNA all over the place. But Shane Grogan's were the only prints on the knife. His clothes were covered in his family's blood. Everybody else had defensive wounds, even the little girl. Grogan had none.' Conor's phone pinged. He glanced at it, frowned, then shoved it in his pocket. 'Okay, I'll give you a very brief summary of the evidence, but then please let it drop. I was hoping I wouldn't have to think about that dreadful case for a few weeks.'

～

Aoife knew it wouldn't be long before Lisa approached her again and, sure enough, Lisa was standing at her car when she finished work.

'How did you know which office I worked in?'

'I called to your house, but Detective Moloney's car was there. I saw your daughter playing outside. The teenage boy she was with told me where you worked.'

'You've got to stop coming to my house, Lisa. You'll get in trouble with the police if you keep harassing us.'

'I'm not harassing you. I just want to talk.'

Aoife unlocked her car. 'Well, we can't talk here. There's a coffee shop at the end of the road. I'll meet you there.'

～

'Did you speak to him?' Lisa asked.

'A cappuccino, please,' Aoife said to the waitress who had approached them.

Lisa ordered a black coffee.

'When did you last eat?' Aoife asked, noticing for the first time how pale Lisa was.

'I don't know. Yesterday, I think. What did Detective Moloney say?'

'Excuse me,' Aoife called back the waitress. 'Could we have a plate of sandwiches as well, please?'

'I'm not hungry.'

'If you don't eat, you'll make yourself sick.'

'I'm fine. Did you speak to Detective Moloney?'

'Yes.'

'Thank you. When will he meet with me?'

'He's not going to meet with you, Lisa. As I said, he's on holidays for a few weeks.'

'What? Didn't you tell him—'

'I told him exactly what you said. Conor understands why you believe your brother is innocent, but he says all the evidence points to Shane's guilt.'

'But that just means the murderer did a very good job of covering his tracks.'

The waitress arrived with a large plate of sandwiches and two coffees. Aoife pushed the plate towards Lisa. 'You need to eat.'

Lisa shook her head. 'There's something the police missed. There has to be.'

'Do you know that the note was in Shane's handwriting?'

'Somebody obviously forced him to write it.'

'And you know Shane didn't have any defensive wounds? Do you think he would have allowed his attacker to cut his wrists without making any attempt to defend himself?'

'He must have been tied up.'

'There are no rope marks. No signs of restraint at all. There's not even one other scratch on his body. Everybody else...' She couldn't bring herself to finish the sentence.

'Their throats were cut, I know that, and you think a murderer would have cut Shane's throat as well but, don't you see, the murder wanted it to look like Shane killed his family. That's why his wrists were cut.'

'Forensics are positive Shane cut his own wrists. Apparently they can tell from the angle and the depth of the cut.'

'Either they're wrong or the murderer figured out a way to fool them.' When Aoife didn't reply, she said, 'Do you have brothers or sisters?'

Aoife shook her head.

'Well, if you did, you would understand what I'm saying. I grew up with Shane. I knew him before he learned to hide the less acceptable facets of his personality. I know what he's capable of.'

'People change. Life happens, we grow up, we become different people.'

'People's attitudes and beliefs change. Their basic nature doesn't. And anyway, I moved in with Shane after my relationship broke up. I lived with them for almost three months while I looked for a place of my own. I'd only moved out two weeks before the murder, and we all had dinner in my mother's house the weekend before. Shane was perfectly normal on Sunday. You're telling me he had turned into a homicidal maniac by Thursday? That isn't possible.'

'I know it's hard to accept, but—'

'I can't accept it because it isn't true. I don't know how the murderer managed to fool the forensic guys, but I am absolutely certain that Shane didn't kill anybody.'

'I don't know what to say, Lisa.'

'I need you to understand.' Lisa sipped her coffee,

then put the mug down with a clatter. 'It's like this. Shane worked for my uncle. My uncle has this big firm that employs an entire sales department, but Shane and my cousin are his top salespeople. They're both outgoing and can talk to anyone, but the difference between them is that Shane has a genuine interest in people. He loves everyone and wants to help them. My cousin is only interested in making money.'

'I don't see what this—'

'The point I'm trying to make is I know my cousin almost as well as I know Shane. Keith spent most of his summers in our house when we were kids, and from as far back as I can remember, he was selfish and sly. He'd steal my toys, pinch me when nobody was looking and get me into trouble any chance he got. He hid that side of himself from the adults and, as he grew older, he learned to hide it from everybody. He's conned people into thinking he's a great person, but I know his basic nature. He's not a nice guy. He never was and he never will be. I doubt he'd murder his wife or his kids, but I'd be prepared to consider it as a possibility. I know Shane even better and it simply isn't in him.' She swallowed. 'It wasn't in him.'

'Even if you're right, Lisa, there's nothing Conor can do to help. He takes his job very seriously and he's investigated everything thoroughly. The evidence just isn't there.'

Lisa reached for her coffee and took a sip. 'I asked around about you and I looked you up. I read the article you wrote about your father-in-law's murder. You were the one who solved that case, not the police.'

'I got lucky.'

'It was more than luck. Aoife, I need your help. If the police can't prove Shane's innocence, I need you to do it.'

'What? No! I'm a journalist, not a detective.'

'You solved one case, you can solve this one.'

'No, Lisa. I'm sorry. I can't. I wouldn't even know where to begin and I can't get involved in a case that Conor is investigating. I could get him into serious trouble.'

'But he's not investigating it. That's the whole point. He's decided Shane is the murderer.'

'Conor says the investigation is ongoing. There are a few loose ends they need to tie up.'

'What loose ends?'

'I don't know.'

'You said Detective Moloney's on holiday. Start your investigation by talking to his replacement and follow up with him. You don't need to involve Detective Moloney at all.'

Aoife shook her head. 'I'm sorry, Lisa. If you want to conduct a private investigation, hire a professional. I can't be involved.'

'I would if I could afford it, but I can't and Mum's had all the funeral expenses. Private investigators charge by the hour and they don't guarantee results. I'll make it worth your while, Aoife. I'll give you an interview.'

'What?'

'That article you wrote about your father-in-law's murder was good for your career, wasn't it? Think how much more attention you would get from interviewing

Shane Grogan's sister. I've had requests for interviews from newspapers and TV stations all over the world. This could make your career.'

Aoife hesitated.

'I promise I will give you a full one-hour interview, family photos, anything you want as soon as you have completed the investigation.'

Aoife put down her coffee. 'What if I find proof your brother was the murderer?'

'You won't, but if you do, I'll still keep my promise. You're the only reporter I will ever speak to.'

'What if I don't find any evidence at all?'

'The interview is dependent on you finding evidence that proves Shane is either guilty or innocent. Either way, you win. Nobody in the family has spoken to the press. I'll make sure they speak to you. You'll still have the basis for a great story.'

Aoife could feel her excitement rising. Her attitude to journalism had changed once Amy was born. She no longer dreamed of being a renowned journalist, all she wanted was a job that allowed her to work from home and brought in enough to pay the bills. Now she felt the tiniest stirring of ambition. International interest was unlikely, but Irish interest was all she needed. It would be a huge boost to her career.

'I have two conditions.'

'Anything.'

'I can't do it unless Conor agrees. I won't risk damaging his career.'

Lisa smiled. 'I'd worry if he was your husband, but boyfriends tend to be on the agreeable side. What's the second condition?'

Aoife nodded at the plate that lay between them. 'You have to eat every one of those sandwiches.'

᷈

'You're sure you're okay with this?'

Conor pushed his hand down the side of the sofa and fished out three coins. 'The detective in me isn't happy about it, but your partner can see it would be good for your career, and I am on holidays for the next few weeks.' His voice was muffled as he stuck his head under the sofa. 'You haven't asked who's taken over my cases while I'm out.'

'Not Derek?'

'Who else? He is my right-hand man.'

Aoife flicked through a pile of magazines. 'Well, I can rule out any hope of getting your replacement to talk to me off the record. Derek isn't exactly the chatty type.'

Conor grinned and she threw a cushion at him. 'You're enjoying this!'

He caught the cushion and tossed it on the sofa before heading for the bookshelves. 'A little bit. I'm not going to try to talk you out of your investigation, but I don't like reporters sticking their noses into my cases. Not even reporters as beautiful as—hey, I found it.' He held up her car key. 'It was behind this book. Amy must have hidden it. We're going to have to hide that stepladder.'

'If there was chocolate up there, Amy might risk it, but

she's afraid of the top step. She wouldn't climb up there for books.'

'It must have been you, then. You're getting very absent-minded lately, honey. Are you okay? Is this case stressing you out already?'

'There's no way I put my keys there.'

'Well, I certainly didn't. Who else is—? You're not saying you think Blaine did it, are you?'

'Who else could it have been?'

Conor's voice hardened. 'Blaine would not do something like that, Aoife. I know you and he have a difficult relationship, but don't blame him because you're absent-minded.'

'You really think I came home, walked through the hall, past the kitchen and my office and came in here to stick my keys behind a book?'

'No, I think you were looking for a book and you absent-mindedly left the keys down on the shelf. You turned the oven off while the dinner was cooking a few days ago too, remember?'

'I don't think that was me.'

'Are you saying Blaine turned off the oven and hid your keys? Why would he do something like that?'

'Because he resents me.'

'He doesn't resent you. He's just not comfortable around you. If you give him time, he'll come around, but not if you start blaming him for every single little thing that goes wrong around here.'

Aoife sighed. 'Let's not fight. Maybe I was wrong.'

VAL COLLINS

Conor didn't reply.

'And I shouldn't have accused Blaine without any evidence. I'm sorry, okay?'

Conor planted a quick kiss on her head and then pulled away. 'You're going to be late for work.'

He walked her to the door and kissed her again but he didn't smile and she could see the worry in his eyes.

EIGHT

THINGS WERE A bit tense between them the following day, but Conor was back to his normal self by the time they went to his work function on Thursday.

Usually Aoife hated those events. Conor's team were too cliquey and they made little attempt to include outsiders in their conversations. The first of Conor's work events Aoife had attended, she'd sat in silence for over thirty minutes while one of the guys did impersonations of people she'd never met while Conor and his friends roared with laughter. It was Derek's wife, Jenny, who'd rescued her. Despite the age difference, they'd become good friends and both regretted that they lived so far apart. It was one of the reasons Jenny had convinced Aoife to join her book club. They would make a night of it, Jenny promised. First they'd go for a few drinks, then book club followed by a late dinner. Aoife had been quite excited and had even tried to talk Orla into joining.

They had been in a Starbucks when Aoife made the suggestion. Orla had laughed so hard she spilled coffee all over her brand-new Stella McCartney top.

'Not my kind of club, Aoife,' she had said when she recovered her breath.

Aoife wished Orla could be with her tonight. She could do with a bit of moral support. As they approached the door of the hotel, she took a deep breath and glanced up at Conor.

'It will be fine. You look great.'

Aoife gave a fake smile. When Conor lifted an eyebrow, she laughed out loud.

Arm in arm, they headed for the function room and almost bumped into Jenny as she came out of the ladies'.

'My God, Aoife! What a dress! It makes me feel old.'

Aoife twirled, aware that Orla's figure-hugging dress showed off curves she hadn't even realised she possessed. 'Do you really think so? Orla lent it to me, but she's so blonde. It's not a colour I'd normally wear.'

'Oh, you're young enough to wear any colour. Now if I tried to wear white, I'd fade into the background. People would think I didn't exist.'

Aoife laughed. 'Anyone would think you were a hundred. You're not old, Jenny.'

'I'll be forty in six months. Of course I'm old. Come on, we kept you a seat.'

Aoife caught the tightening of Conor's mouth. 'Why don't we mingle for a while first? Any newbies?'

'Two or three. They look very young. I wouldn't be

surprised if most of them are first dates. We'll probably never see them again.' She poked Conor with her elbow. 'You lot would scare anybody off.'

'What are you talking about, Jenny?' Conor said in mock outrage. 'You could not find a nicer, friendlier bunch of guys anywhere.'

'Hmm.'

'Hmm, indeed,' Aoife said. 'You look very smart, Jenny. I love your hair.'

'Thanks. I had to do something to make up for having to wear the same dress for the hundredth time.' She patted her updo. 'The colour came out rather well, didn't it? There's nothing worse than badly dyed blonde hair.'

Aoife made a gesture to Conor. He squeezed her arm and slipped away. It was always a challenge enjoying Jenny's company at these events while making sure Conor didn't get stuck with Derek. This time she wanted Conor to stay away as long as possible. She was hoping she could get Derek to relax enough to discuss Shane Grogan's case before he learned Aoife planned to investigate it.

They spent a few minutes introducing themselves to the newest additions to the group, then Jenny led Aoife back to the table Derek was holding for them.

'Hi, Aoife.' Derek stood, extended his hand and smiled. He was always very formal. At last summer's barbecue, he had turned up in a suit and tie. Tonight all the guys wore suits. To mark the formality of the occasion, Derek had added a waistcoat and a bow tie.

'I love the tie, Derek.'

Derek smiled and straightened the emerald-green bow tie that was the exact shade of Jenny's dress.

'The girls gave it to him as a Christmas present. He's been waiting for an opportunity to wear it ever since. Aoife, would you mind taking our photo? I'll send it to the girls. They'll love it.'

Aoife examined the photo before handing the phone back. 'You both look very smart. And that dress may not be new, Jenny, but it really suits you.'

'Derek thinks it's too revealing.'

'You must think my dress is shocking then.' Aoife smiled at Derek, willing him to join in the conversation.

'Your dress is very beautiful, Aoife, and I wouldn't presume to tell any woman how she should dress, especially my wife.'

Jenny smiled. 'You don't need to say anything, darling. I saw the way you looked at it when I put it on. I have gained a bit of weight lately and it's a tiny bit too tight, but compared to most of the young girls here, I'm dressed like a grandmother.'

'If so, you're the most beautiful, glamorous grandmother I've ever seen.'

'Ah! You two are so sweet!'

Jenny laughed and leaned back against her husband. 'I found myself a good one when I picked you, Derek Lehane.'

As they chatted, Aoife noticed that all the detectives stopped to say hello and shake Derek's hand. Not one stayed to chat. Aoife's phone beeped. 'Sorry, I just have to check this.'

The text was from Conor. 'Want me to rescue you?' She gave a quick reply. 'Fine here. Enjoying talking to Jenny. See you later.'

'Is everything okay?' Derek asked.

Aoife nodded. 'I just had to check in case anything was wrong with Amy.'

'Of course,' Derek said. 'We always worry about our girls too. Especially now our eldest is a teenager.'

'They grow up so fast, don't they?' Aoife sipped the drink Jenny had bought her. 'Amy's in preschool now. She'll be starting school in two years' time. Jason thinks she should start next year, but I'd rather wait until she's five.'

'Where are you sending her?' Derek asked.

'I don't know yet. I've her name down for half a dozen schools, but there are so many things to consider. I'd prefer she went to a private school, but her dad's not keen. Even Conor doesn't seem to think it's a good idea.'

'Our girls started off in the local national school, but they're going to the convent now.'

'But don't make the mistake we made,' Derek said. 'If I were you, Aoife, I'd put her straight into the convent. I've seen what goes on with young kids these days, and the longer you can keep her away from boys, the better.'

Jenny grinned at Aoife. 'This is what happens when you marry a policeman. They see danger everywhere. If Derek had his way, the girls would have a police escort every time they left the house.'

Derek smiled. 'I can't say I wouldn't like it. But, as that's not an option, the convent's the next best thing.'

'Wouldn't Amy be better off in a mixed school, at least until she reaches her teens, especially as she has no brothers?'

'That's what I thought,' Jenny said. 'And it's why the girls went to a mixed primary school, but Derek thinks we made a mistake. Caoimhe decided this boy in her class was her "boyfriend" when she was eleven. She's fourteen now and they still claim they're in love.'

'That's my point,' Derek said. 'Fourteen is far too young to have a serious boyfriend, and Caoimhe would never have met him if she'd gone to the convent from the beginning.'

'She'll probably get tired of him pretty soon and move on to some other young lad.'

Derek frowned. 'I doubt it. Caoimhe's her mother's daughter. Once she commits to somebody or something, she'll stick with it to the bitter end.'

'The bitter end! My God, Derek. Don't be so gloomy. Come on, let's dance.'

'Jenny, no! You know I'm a terrible dancer.'

'Anyone can slow-dance. Just put your arms around me and shift from one foot to the other. You'll be fine.'

She dragged a reluctant Derek onto the dance floor. Aoife was just thinking Derek had quite a good sense of rhythm when two hands landed on her shoulder. 'Come on! Quick!' Conor led her on to the dance floor.

She put both her arms around his neck and swayed to the music. 'You know you can't avoid Derek all night?'

'I know. I'll go back to the table with you. Mike's promised to rescue me after fifteen minutes. Give me a sign if you need a break, and I'll tell them I have to introduce you to somebody.'

'No, I don't get enough opportunity to talk to Jenny, and Derek is okay. He's not exactly the life of the party, but he means well.'

'Yeah, I know.' Conor waved at Derek and Jenny as they left the dance floor. 'I'm glad he's on my team, but I can't spend an entire night with him. He's so proper, I have to censor all our conversations. Last year I said one of the lads was driving me crazy and Derek looked shocked. He said the guy's wife had just given birth to twins and, very subtly because he never forgets I'm his boss, gave me a ten-minute lecture on tolerance.'

Aoife laughed. 'That will teach you.'

'He was right, of course, but I haven't been able to have a non-work-related conversation with him since. I can't live up to his standards.'

Aoife drew away to look at him. 'That's it! I've been trying to work out the dynamics between Derek and the team. He's like the grandfather, isn't he? He's not in charge, so he doesn't feel the need to be involved. Everybody respects him, but they'd rather play with their friends.'

'Oh my God! You see us as little boys?'

'Not you. You're more like an older brother—older and wiser than your years but you're still one of the lads.' She nodded over at a group of Conor's colleagues who were now nudging each other and pointing at a young girl a few tables away. 'When some of that lot have a few drinks on them, they act like ten-year-olds.'

Conor laughed. Drawing her closer, he said, 'You may have a point there, but it might be as well not to say it too loudly.'

They stayed on the dance floor until it got to the stage where their continued absence might be viewed as a deliberate attempt to avoid Derek and Jenny. Derek stood as Conor approached and offered his hand.

'Detective Inspector.'

'Conor, please. We're not on duty now, Derek. I've never seen you dance before. You've been holding out on us.'

'Thank you!' Jenny said. 'I've been trying to convince him he's a good dancer for years.'

'My dancing years are far behind me, darling.'

'Derek Lehane, in the sixteen years we've been married, the only time you voluntarily danced with me was on our wedding day. When exactly were your dancing years?'

Derek smiled but he didn't reply. 'This might be a good time for me to give you an update on your cases, Detective.'

Aoife held her breath, but Conor shook his head. 'I don't think this is the place, Derek.'

'Oh, don't worry about me,' Jenny said. 'Derek tells me everything.'

'Really? Conor doesn't even mention his work to me.'

'I don't tell you everything, darling.' Derek looked a little uncomfortable. 'I answer your questions.'

Aoife sniffed. 'Conor certainly doesn't answer mine.'

'Well, you're not married yet. Jenny and I have been a team for a long time. She takes care of our kids, our finances and'—he patted his slightly protruding stomach—'my middle-aged spread. I know I can trust her not to talk about my work.'

'You don't trust me, Conor?'

'I trust my partner,' he said. 'I'm not so sure about the reporter.'

'You're a reporter? Jenny said you worked in an office.'

'I'm a part-time office worker and a part-time freelance journalist.'

Derek gave her a wary look. 'That's completely different. It's a conflict of interest. It's something that will always be between you, I'm afraid.'

'I'm sure they'll work it out, Derek. Come on, Aoife. Let's go to the bar and have a drink. We'll leave these two to discuss their cases in peace.'

'They'll be discussing the Grogan case,' Aoife said when they had finally managed to attract the barman's attention. 'How well did you know Shane?'

'Not very well. He hardly ever came to our meetings. Fiona must have talked him into joining. I think he felt odd being the only guy in the group.'

'I often meant to ask you about that. Why aren't there any guys?'

'It was originally set up as a women's literary fiction group, and I guess that doesn't have a lot of appeal for men.'

'Did Fiona come to the meetings often?'

'About once every three or four months. She was

desperate to join a book club, but I don't think ours would have been her first choice. She didn't really share our taste in books. Whenever she turned up, she tried to convert us to genre fiction. It's a good thing Ruth wasn't at most of those meetings. Blood would have been shed.' Jenny covered her mouth with both hands. 'I can't believe I said that.'

Aoife winced. 'It doesn't bear thinking about.' She sipped her drink. 'I didn't even know Conor and Derek were investigating the case. Did you?'

'Yes. A case like that wouldn't go to anybody else. Conor is the lead investigator. He gets all the big cases.'

Aoife felt a tiny glow of pride. 'He is very good at his job.'

'They both are.'

'Yes, of course. I didn't mean—'

Jenny put a hand on Aoife's arm. 'Don't mind me. I'm prickly where Derek is concerned. Mostly guilt, I think.'

'Guilt?'

'I was the one who talked Derek into moving to Dublin. If he'd stayed in Limerick, he'd be the one in charge.'

'You couldn't have lived in Bodyke forever, Jenny. It's barely a village.'

'I know, although Derek's commute was a lot shorter than it is now. Still, if we'd stayed there, the girls would have left home at seventeen and we'd barely ever see them again. Now they'll live with us while they're in college and probably until they're a few years in their first job. It was the best decision for the family, but sometimes I wonder if I gave enough thought to Derek's feelings.'

'Derek is a detective in Harcourt Street. Every detective in the country would kill to work there. You can't compare it to a garda station in Limerick.'

'He's a small fish in a big, flashy pond. It's not the same as being in charge, is it? Sometimes I wonder if he resents me.'

'That's silly, Jenny. Anybody can see he adores you, and sometimes you have to take a step back in your career in order to move forward. It will all work out in the end.'

'I hope you're right.'

'Conor said Derek did a brilliant interview last time and, according to one of the interview panel, there were only two points between them. Derek almost became the Detective Inspector. The next time there's a promotion, he's bound to get it.'

'I really hope so. Derek's career is very important to him.'

'It's always difficult when you feel your career has stalled. Or in my case, when it's barely started. Although I have some good news. I've been offered an exclusive interview with the Grogan family.'

'That's brilliant, Aoife. I'm glad to see you pushing ahead with journalism. How did you get them to speak to you? I thought they refused to give any interviews.'

'They're doing it in return for me finding Shane's killer.'

'But Shane killed himself.'

'His sister doesn't think so.'

'Yes, well, I can understand that. I barely knew him

and I was absolutely stunned. Shane was always so happy and outgoing. Not at all the lunatic type.'

'I'm going to have to interview everyone they ever spoke to. I thought I'd start with the book club.'

'You want to interview me?'

'At some stage, yes. Or do you want to do it now?'

Jenny glanced over at Derek. 'They look very serious. I think they'll be there for a while.' She put her drink down on the bar. 'Ask away.'

'What can you tell me about Shane?'

'He hated literary fiction, and I never heard him say a single negative thing about any member of his family.'

'What did he say about them?'

'Not much. His eldest wanted a dog for Christmas, but Fiona wasn't keen on the idea. He asked me if we had ever considered getting a dog and if I thought they would be a lot of work. Once he said his god-daughter was turning thirteen and what did teenage girls like these days. Other than that...' Jenny shrugged. 'He only came to the book club a few times.'

'When was the last time you saw him?'

'A few weeks before the murder. It was their turn to host the book club, so they were both there. Fiona had spent months trying to talk us into reading *Gone with the Wind* and that was the week we were discussing it. When she was a teenager, she had got all caught up in the romance of it and she still loved it. Shane said it was racist crap. The discussion started on WhatsApp, but it almost got out of control at the meeting. I thought some people were going to come to blows. In the middle, Shane disappeared and came back with a birthday cake and champagne. It was the day before Fiona's fortieth. We had a small, impromptu party. It was a nice evening. I really enjoyed it.' She laughed. 'Actually, I enjoyed it a bit too much. I was on my third glass of champagne before I remembered I was driving. I had to get Derek to collect me.'

The bartender passed them and Jenny motioned that they would like a refill.

'You know, Aoife, the more I think of that night, the harder it is for me to believe Shane could have killed Fiona, let alone the kids.' She shrugged. 'But I guess you can't ever know another person or what's really going on in their minds.'

'Do you have photos of the party?'

Jenny took out her phone and opened WhatsApp. She quickly flicked through a bunch of photos. 'Here.'

In all there were about twenty photos. Different groups of women smiling for the camera. There were two group photos, one of women with their arms around each other, laughing into the camera, and another of them raising champagne flutes while sitting on a sofa, balancing plates of cake on their knees.

'Which one is Fiona?'

'She isn't there. These are the photos she took. Shane took some of us too, but I don't know where they ended up.'

'Do you have a photo of Shane?'

Jenny flicked through the pictures and handed the phone to Aoife. Shane was better looking than Aoife had imagined. He had Lisa's chocolate-brown hair, and his eyes were a grey-blue colour. He held a champagne bottle in one hand and was leaning over Jenny's shoulder to get into the photo. Jenny was holding up a knife that had bits of chocolate cake stuck to it. Both their mouths formed an 'o'.

'Were you singing?' Aoife asked.

Jenny looked at the photo and gave a sad smile. 'Yes. Shane forgot to get birthday candles, but he had one of those huge round candles left over from Christmas. I cut the cake, Shane popped the champagne, Jenny blew out the candle, and we all sang "Happy Birthday."' She picked up her drink. 'I've looked at that photo so many times, trying to see if there was anything in Shane's eyes that I missed.'

'He looks a lot younger than forty.'

'He was thirty-four. Fiona used to joke she was the only one of us who had a toy boy.'

'Is there anybody in the book club who knew them well?'

'A lot of us knew Fiona, but not Shane. Ruth might be able to tell you about him. She vets all the members. The first time I met her, she said, "Oh, the detective's wife. I hope you're not into thrillers." If there was anything worth knowing about Shane and Fiona, you can be sure Ruth has all the details.'

Mike came to rescue Conor, and Aoife and Jenny returned to the table. The wary look on Derek's face settled any doubts Aoife had that he now knew of her planned investigation. There was no chance of getting information from

Derek tonight. She would arrange an official meeting for next week. In the meantime, she would work on trying to establish a more relaxed relationship with Derek.

'What made you decide to join the police force, Derek?'

'It's something I've wanted to do since I was a child.'

'What appealed to you about it?'

Derek put his palms together as if he was about to pray. He thought for a few minutes, then said, 'At first, it was just a kid's dream, but as I got older, I realised that all the problems in the world were because people don't obey the law. If nobody ever committed any crimes, the world would be such a peaceful place. Obviously, that will never happen, but I want to do my bit to improve the world by ridding it of as many law-breakers as possible. Of course, in our current system, I can only send them on to the courts, and half the time they're released in a few years, but if people like me didn't try, what kind of a place would the world be?'

'So you want to make the world a better place?'

Derek nodded. 'Better, and also safer for my family and every other family out there.'

'When you think about it, our jobs are pretty similar, aren't they?'

Derek frowned. 'In what way?'

'We both investigate crimes. We both try to make sure criminals are brought to justice and innocent people are safe in their homes.'

'The difference, Aoife, is that the police are trained to handle investigations. Journalists make our jobs harder.'

'I certainly have no intention of making your job harder.'

'The best way to achieve that is by staying out of the investigation. As Detective Inspector Moloney's future wife, I want to offer you all possible assistance. Therefore, when we have apprehended the murderer, I'll tell you everything I'm at liberty to share with the public and you will have ample information to write a great article several hours before the information is released to the press.'

'Perhaps we could have a brief meeting first? Conor and I have decided it's best we never discuss this case. I was hoping you could go over the facts with me sometime next week.'

Derek nodded. 'Of course. Any information Detective Inspector Moloney clears me to share with you, I'll be very happy to pass it on.'

NINE

MORNINGS WERE ALWAYS a rush for Aoife, so as
soon as she came home from work, she changed her clothes
and left out her outfit for the following day. The two rooms
Amy was drawn to were Aoife's bedroom and her office.
Aoife had put a latch on the office door that Amy couldn't
reach. She didn't want to deny Amy her bedroom, so she
had put a similar latch on the door of the spare room and
laid her clothes out each night on the bare mattress.

It had been after midnight on Thursday when Aoife
got home from Conor's function. Friday morning, she slept
through her alarm. As soon as she woke, Aoife jumped out
of bed and ran to the shower. Four minutes later, barefoot
and wrapped in a towel, she unlatched the door of the spare
room. She blinked twice before it registered. The only thing
on the bed was a pair of socks. Blaine had struck again.

Aoife dug through the ironing hamper until she found
something crumpled but clean. She dropped off Amy at

kindergarten and arrived at the Kildare library just as Lisa approached.

The library was one of Aoife's regular haunts. She waved at the librarians as she passed and led Lisa to a long table in a secluded corner. She didn't know Lisa well enough to invite her to her home, so the library seemed the best option. They had at least an hour before the local primary school kids arrived to choose their book of the week, and they were unlikely to be disturbed by the older kids who had already started their summer holidays. Aoife switched on her computer.

'So, what's the first thing we do?' Lisa asked.

There was an energy to her voice that Aoife hadn't heard before. She took in Lisa's shining hair and the carefully applied make-up. 'You look very different.'

Lisa smiled. 'When I told Mum you would investigate the murder, she was so relieved we went into town to celebrate. We had lunch in Café en Seine and afterwards we had massages and got our hair done. It was the happiest I've seen her since everything went haywire.'

'I'm glad you had a good day.'

'Yes, well, you have to grab a bit of peace wherever you can find it. Tell me, Aoife, what can I do to help?'

'I got your list of the people in Shane's life. I think it's best to start with those Shane had most contact with and work my way down, but first I wanted to ask you something. Is it possible Shane had some connection with organised crime?'

'No, of course not!'

'Could he have had a gambling problem?'

'Absolutely not.'

'How can you be sure?'

'Now his family are gone, my mother is his next of kin. I've been handling the paperwork. He had a mortgage on the house and two years left on a car loan, but he had no other debts.'

'You won't find any paper records for the kind of debts that would get your family murdered.'

'Shane wasn't a gambler, Aoife. I'm certain of it.'

Aoife put an asterisk beside the word 'gambling'. Something to follow up with Derek.

'Okay, Lisa. The people who saw the most of Shane were your uncle that he worked for and your cousin Keith. Can you arrange for me to meet them?'

Lisa hesitated, then took out her phone. 'Hi, Angela, does my uncle have many appointments this morning?' She waited. 'Eleven-thirty sounds great.'

Lisa's uncle Eamonn was a small man, teetering on the edge of obesity. Having offered them tea or coffee, he started by saying, 'I don't entirely agree with my niece. I've known Shane all his life and he was the last person in the world I would have believed capable of such a terrible act, but I can't imagine anybody else would want to kill the family either.'

Aoife turned to a new page on her notebook. 'Can you tell me something about Shane's role in your organisation?'

'He was my top sales person.'

'Your sales manager?'

'No, that's my son, Keith.'

'Was Shane capable of taking on a management role?'

'Oh yes, the customers loved him. We all did. And he would have made a good manager. He mentored most of the new sales staff and he really brought out the best in them. Many of them became our top performers.'

'If Shane was capable of management, why did he work for a company where he could never fill a management role?'

Eamonn shifted in his seat and glanced at Lisa. 'Is this relevant?'

'Maybe not, but I have to start somewhere. I need to get a picture of Shane's life; what his financial situation was like, did he have any enemies, that kind of thing.'

'He didn't have any enemies that I know of, and he was on good money, so I doubt he had debts.'

'How come he never moved to a company with promotional opportunities?'

'He—I suppose it doesn't make much difference now'—Eamonn looked at Lisa—'but this has to stay between us.'

Lisa nodded.

'A few years ago, Shane was offered the position of sales manager with a rival firm.'

'He never mentioned it to me,' Lisa said.

'I asked him not to tell anybody. We came to an agreement. I told Shane I couldn't make him a sales manager but I'd give him the title of senior sales consultant and he would report directly to me. I also agreed he would have the same salary and bonus package as Keith.'

'I take it your son is unaware of this arrangement.'

'Yes, and I want it to stay that way.'

'It wasn't a long-term solution, though, was it? You must have known Shane would move on eventually.'

Eamonn glanced at the door and lowered his voice. 'I promised Shane that, on my death, he and Keith would be joint owners of the business.'

TEN

AOIFE DROVE DOWN the road in a daze. Her very first interview and she'd found the killer already? Things like that didn't happen in real life. They didn't even happen that often in fiction.

'Are you as shocked as I am?' she said at last.

'Huh? Sorry, Aoife, I was miles away. What did you say?'

'I said I'm shocked that we have a suspect after just one interview.'

'My uncle!'

'No, Keith. You said he wasn't a nice guy. Now we know he had a motive for killing Shane.'

'He might have a motive, but he didn't kill Shane. He's the sneaky, underhand sort. I know he tried to turn my uncle against Shane, and there's nothing he wanted more than to get Shane out of the company, but slitting some-one's throat? He wouldn't have the stomach for it. And what possible reason could he have for murdering Shane's family? They were part of his family too.'

'Jealousy, fury? Maybe he regretted it afterwards but it was too late. You need to make an appointment for me to interview him.'

'Mmm.' Lisa picked at a chipped fingernail.

'Lisa?'

'Look, I know I promised you everybody in the family would speak to you, and I'm working on that, but at the moment Keith's refusing to be involved.'

'Why?'

'His exact response was, "You are completely insane and I don't have time to waste on this nonsense".'

'Are those the words of an innocent man?'

'Probably. They're also the words of a selfish, inconsiderate bastard.'

'Okay, suppose you're right and Keith isn't the murderer. Who else is there?'

Lisa shook her head. 'I wish I knew.'

⤫

Conor and Blaine came for dinner as usual that evening. Aoife was determined to keep Blaine out of the house as much as possible.

'There's no need to help me, Conor. Dinner is almost ready.'

'If you're sure. Hey, Blaine! Do you want to practice your pucks?'

Ever since Blaine had learned his father had once played

in the All Ireland Junior Hurling Final, he had become obsessed with the game. There were no GAA clubs near his home in England, so he and Conor practised every day during Blaine's visits.

Aoife watched them for a few minutes. She returned to the kitchen, relieved that for a short period she didn't have to worry what Blaine was up to. Once the dinner was finished, Aoife was on full alert and followed Blaine every time he left the room.

'Are you alright?' Conor asked.

'Yes, why?'

'You're very on edge. You haven't sat down for more than a few minutes all evening.'

'I've been sitting down the whole day. I'm dying for some exercise.' She jumped up. 'Come on! Blaine hasn't been here in the summer before. It's time he saw the Curragh at its best.'

They walked for two hours and Aoife quite enjoyed the evening. Blaine had put Amy on his shoulders. Amy was thrilled to have found a new horsie, a role usually fulfilled by Conor. She insisted Blaine gallop up and down the fields. It almost felt like Aoife and Conor were alone at last.

'Blaine is settling in now, isn't he?' Conor said.

Aoife couldn't bring herself to point out that Blaine was playing Amy's game mostly so he could have as little interaction with Aoife as possible.

'I hope so,' she said and changed the subject.

When Conor and Blaine left, Aoife checked every room in the house. Nothing was missing.

ELEVEN

THE FOLLOWING MORNING, Aoife woke up before her alarm and stretched out in the bed. It was amazing how relaxed she felt, knowing she wasn't in for any nasty surprises for once.

The little bubble of happiness banished any worries she had about her first official meeting with Derek. It was true they didn't know each other well and Derek obviously distrusted reporters, but she was Jenny's friend and Derek had great faith in Jenny's judgement. If she could just get him to relax, he could be a mine of information.

The bubble burst when she was left in the waiting room for over fifteen minutes. When Derek arrived, he offered his hand but did not smile or apologise for keeping her waiting. Was this what he was normally like at work? In comparison, the Derek at the function had been positively jolly.

Aoife had often seen movies where the police were

called away urgently mid-meeting and the investigator had the opportunity to look through confidential files. If such things happened in reality, there was no chance it would happen today. Derek had taken her to a meeting room where the only furnishings were a metal table with unsteady legs and two uncomfortable chairs. The room smelled old and damp and the light green paint had an institutional sheen.

Derek opened a thin manila folder and removed a single typed sheet. In a robotic voice, he began, 'The 999 helpline received a phone call on—'

'Derek, would it be okay if I asked you some questions?'

Looking a little put out, Derek closed his folder. 'Please go ahead.'

'First, can you be certain the murderer wasn't a stranger?'

Derek considered her question, then replied, 'Yes.'

'Can you elaborate?'

'I understand Detective Inspector Moloney explained why we believe Grogan murdered his family. All I can add is that if there was a homicidal maniac wandering the country murdering families, we would have heard about it by now.'

'Is it possible Shane Grogan had a gambling problem and the murders were retaliation for unpaid debts?'

Derek opened the file again and scribbled a note. Was he writing down her questions?

'I can neither confirm nor deny any possible lines of enquiry.'

'Have you interviewed Shane's cousin, Keith?'

More scribbling. 'I can neither confirm nor deny any questions regarding possible witnesses or suspects.'

'Are you aware that Shane's uncle promised to make Shane a part owner in his company and that he kept this information secret from Keith?'

Derek looked up. 'He—I can neither confirm nor deny any possible lines of enquiry.'

His face coloured at the realisation that Aoife had registered his surprise.

'Have you spoken to the members of Fiona's book club?'

He was writing again. 'I can neither confirm nor deny any questions regarding possible witnesses or suspects.'

This was getting her nowhere. Maybe Derek would relax if they could talk in a more informal setting. Closing her notebook, she said, 'Thank you for your help, Derek. Are you planning to get a bite to eat? I'm starving.'

'I brought in my lunch. I'll be eating it at my desk.'

'You'd be doing me a favour by keeping me company. You can eat your sandwich any time.'

'Jenny always gives me a full lunch. All I have to do is put it in the microwave.'

'Lucky you. Well, I'm starving, so I have to get out of here. Thanks for your time, Derek.'

What was she going to do now? Would Jenny put in a good word for her?

✧

Aoife felt quite dejected as she headed for her car. She'd travelled all the way to Dublin for her meeting with Derek, and it had been a complete waste of time. She'd achieved absolutely nothing. Whatever had given her the idea she could be a successful journalist? Didn't all journalists worth their salt have police sources they could rely on?

Her humour lifted when she got a text from Ruth. For the last two weeks, Aoife had been attempting to set up an interview with Ruth. It had taken several days before Ruth had even returned her call. Then she had come up with multiple excuses why she couldn't possibly meet on any of Aoife's suggested dates. Finally, Aoife agreed to meet her anywhere at any time of the day or night. Ruth had promised to get in touch. Aoife had waited a few days, then followed up with a text. Two days later, she'd sent another text, repeating her willingness to meet Ruth any time, any place. Just as Aoife was beginning to believe this whole investigation was a waste of time, Ruth replied to her text. She would meet Aoife the following morning.

Her enthusiasm renewed, Aoife decided it was time to talk to Keith. Lisa had told her that Keith's wife was sick, so he would have to do the school run all week. Aoife arrived at the school fifteen minutes before classes ended. A group of parents stood outside the gates chatting. Several sat waiting in their cars. Aoife searched for the licence plate Lisa had given her. As she walked by, she deliberately stumbled and fell against the driver's window. A startled Keith looked up from his phone.

'Sorry,' Aoife mouthed. She took one step and stumbled again, banging against the back passenger window.

Keith got out of the car. He was about average height,

taller than his father but almost as broad and already carrying more weight than was healthy for a man of his age. He looked at Aoife suspiciously and sniffed the air.

'Are you okay?'

'I'm not feeling too well.' Aoife clutched her stomach. 'I guess this little one wants to make his presence known.' She grabbed the roof of the car as if to steady herself. 'Would you mind if I sat down for just a minute?'

Keith looked around. A few of the mothers were watching them curiously. He opened the back passenger door. Aoife made a big production of sitting down. She sighed. 'Thank you so much.' She put her head between her knees.

Keith stood on the pavement, one hand on the open door.

Aoife sat back against the seat. 'This is much better. Thank you.'

Keith nodded.

'Are you waiting for your children?'

'Yes. Are you?'

'I'm collecting my daughter. What class are your kids in?'

Keith talked about his kids, their classes and their teachers. Aoife nodded and feigned interest.

'I love your car. It's so comfortable. I've always wanted a BMW.'

Keith patted the roof. 'This is my baby.'

'My husband just started in a sales job and I thought all salesmen were given great cars, but Don's car is a Renault and it's six years old. I was shocked.'

'He should move to a larger company. Most companies lease their cars, so it's no trouble to change them every year. This is a company car. Not all our cars are quite this good, but they are all new.'

'Do they have any sales vacancies?'

'Not right now. It's my family company, actually, which is why my car is a little better than the norm. We might have a vacancy in a few months. We are one salesperson down and my father wants to recruit a replacement, but I don't think it's the right time.'

'You're obviously the one in charge, then, as the position isn't advertised yet.'

Keith smiled. 'I wouldn't go that far. The company will be mine someday.' He frowned.

'You don't look too happy at the prospect.'

'Oh, I am. I've given my entire life to our business. I was just thinking how close I came to losing it.'

'How do you mean?'

'Oh nothing. Families, you know how it is. At one stage there were other members of the family interested in my job, but they've lost interest now and it's just me and my father.'

'How did you get out of there?'

'I said I was feeling better. Then the kids came piling out of the school and I pretended one of them was mine. I stopped a little girl and asked her what class she was in and Keith drove past while we were speaking. The important thing, Lisa, is Keith made it clear he knew about his father's will.'

'He actually said Shane was in my uncle's will?'

'Not exactly, but he made it clear he felt his position in the company was threatened by a member of the family and that he believes the family member is no longer a threat.'

'I could see him arguing with Shane. I could see him punching him. I don't see him killing Shane's entire family.'

'There are only two possible reasons the family was murdered in that dreadful way. One is as a warning to others if, for example, organised crime was involved. The other is anger. You would have to be pretty furious to do something so vicious. Does Keith have anger issues?'

'He's always had a temper, but that wasn't mere temper, Aoife. That was sheer lunacy.'

TWELVE

AOIFE HAD ARRANGED to take a day's holidays from work. Maura had happily agreed to collect Amy from kindergarten so Aoife could spend the entire day in Dublin. After her meeting with Ruth, she would have lunch with Orla and the afternoon would be spent interviewing the three members of the book club who had agreed to meet her at short notice.

There was no easy way to get to Rathmines by public transport, so Aoife had to brave the rush-hour traffic. As she inched along the crowded streets, Aoife thought about her relationship with Blaine. She couldn't insist they go for a walk every day, and could she really watch Blaine every minute he was in her house? Conor had full run of the house and Aoife had encouraged Blaine to treat it as his home. It was too late to change her approach now.

At long last, Aoife reached Rathmines. She hadn't been there in years, but she remembered it well. Traditionally known as 'flat land', ever since the 1930s it had been the place where most young people started their lives in Dublin. At all hours of the day and night, the streets had been crammed with young people milling around. Within walking distance of the city centre, it was a handy first stop for students and young people up from the country for their first job. Most moved on after a few years, but for generations, there had been a constant influx of young people to fill the tiny bedsits and two-bedroom flats that were jammed into the crumbling Victorian mansions. Aoife and Orla had often visited the area when they were teenagers. They had loved the energy and youthful vibe and enjoyed checking out the local shops where everything was sold in the smallest quantities imaginable. It was even possible to buy a single egg.

Like many places in Ireland, the area had been completely changed by the property boom. It was still busy and there were many young people, but the youthful buzz was gone. The occasional crumbling mansion remained, but an astonishing number had been converted to outrageously expensive single-family homes.

Ruth's house was in Leinster Square, a small cul-de-sac set slightly off the main Rathmines Road. Aoife had recognised the address immediately. The top floor had once been occupied by art students who had turned the entire building into a mural, painted every colour under the sun. Once the front door had been left open and Orla and Aoife had marvelled at the artwork on the stairs. Every step was devoted to a different musician. They had time to see a life-size drawing of Bruce Springsteen and read the first line written beneath—'I come from down in the valley where mister when you're young'—before the door had been slammed shut. Aoife had imagined Ruth living in a more upmarket version of the building she remembered, perhaps with the artists replaced by authors. She couldn't have been more wrong.

In contrast to the dilapidated house of Aoife's memory, Ruth's home was pristine. The outside walls were painted a brilliant white, and the small front garden that had once held overflowing rubbish bins was now paved and occupied by a people carrier and a small Ford Fiesta. The Fiesta was a bit of a surprise. Why would somebody living in a house that must have cost at least three million drive a Fiesta? She'd expected a Jag or at least a Volvo. Maybe it belonged to the help.

As she was about to ring the doorbell, the door was flung open and a boy of about ten burst out. Seeing her startled expression, he stood back to let her enter. Before slamming the door after him, he shouted, 'Mum! Visitors.'

Aoife tried to go outside again and ring the doorbell, but the door had locked automatically and she couldn't figure out how to open it. She was alone in a narrow corridor with high ceilings and ornate plasterwork. The walls were cream and bare. Not even a single painting adorned them.

'Hello!' she called, but there was no answer. There were rooms on either side of the corridor, but the doors were shut and her knocking elicited no response. She pulled out her mobile.

'Hi, Ruth, this is Aoife. Your son let me into the house. I'm standing in the hall at the moment.'

'On my way.'

Aoife heard a door in the basement bang and footsteps on the stairs. Aoife hadn't seen Ruth since her first night at the book club, but she was pretty sure Ruth had lost weight. Her tiny frame was so fragile it looked like a strong wind could knock her over.

'I'm sorry,' Ruth said, her brown curls bopping up and down as she hurried towards Aoife. 'Boys are unbelievably rude, aren't they?' She looked around. 'Are you on your own?'

'Yes.'

'Please, follow me.' She led the way down a narrow staircase.

The entire basement had been converted into an enormous kitchen. It came as a bit of a shock to see another room without a single splash of colour. Aoife thought it was a shame Ruth had chosen the metallic, dark grey cupboards that were now so fashionable. The room also had a Belfast sink, another popular feature that Aoife hated. Black marble countertops ran both sides of the room and were covered with an impressive array of electrical gadgets. Aoife spotted a yoghurt maker and popcorn popper. She thought she recognised a food dehydrator, and one of the gadgets looked similar to an egg cooker she'd seen on TV. After pushing several buttons on something that looked complicated enough to launch nuclear missiles but, judging by the coffee mugs standing nearby, was probably a percolator, Ruth led her into the conservatory, which took up most of what had once been a narrow, rectangular garden. The room was L-shaped. A long dining table filled the centre, and the room opened up into a cosy seating area overlooking a miniscule but beautifully landscaped garden. A middle-aged man removed his glasses, folded his newspaper, tossed it on the table and stood to greet her.

'This is Martin.'

In stark contrast to Ruth's pink Juicy Couture tracksuit and runners that looked like they had never seen the outdoors, Martin was dressed in a suit and tie.

'Pleased to meet you,' he said. 'Please sit down.'

Aoife sat in one of the single chairs, Ruth took the chair opposite and Martin remained on the sofa. Martin and Ruth glanced at each other but neither spoke.

'You have a lovely home,' Aoife said.

'Thank you. Sometimes I think it was a waste converting the entire house when we spend most of our time in the basement. Well, the kids and the nanny use the playroom upstairs, but I hardly ever set foot in it.'

They exchanged glances again and Martin cleared his throat.

'Will Detective Moloney be joining us?'

'No. You do understand I'm not a member of the police force?'

'Yes, but as you are Detective Moloney's fiancée, we expected him to accompany you.'

Aoife cringed at the term but didn't correct him.

'No, I'm on my own.'

'Ruth and I don't know why either you or the police are interested in speaking to us. There's nothing we can tell you about the Grogan murders.'

'I understand, but I'm speaking to everyone who knew the family.'

'We didn't know them very well. Shane and I used to coach the local rugby team, but I stopped that years ago when it became obvious my boys had no interest in the sport. I hadn't spoken to Shane in several years.'

This was better than Aoife had expected. 'How many years did you coach together?'

'About four.'

Aoife looked at Ruth. 'So you both knew Shane quite well?'

'Not very well,' they both said at the same time.

Ruth nodded at Martin, who continued. 'Shane was in the house a few times, but we never discussed our personal lives and, as I said, I hadn't spoken to him in years.'

'And you, Ruth? When was the last time you and Shane spoke?'

'I don't remember, exactly.'

'Has he been to your house in the last twelve months?'

'Maybe. I can't be certain.'

'So you stayed friendly with him although your husband didn't?'

Ruth bristled. 'As you know, Fiona was in my book club. I mentioned I was having trouble with my heating system and she sent Shane around to fix it. I can't remember exactly when that was, but it was a few months before the murder.'

Martin shifted in his seat.

'And you weren't in the house on that occasion, Martin?' Aoife asked.

'No, if I had been, Ruth wouldn't have needed to ask somebody else for help.' There was an edge to his voice.

Ruth rolled her eyes. 'Of course you were always so handy when you…' She gave Aoife a smile that didn't reach her eyes. 'I'm sorry, you don't need to hear us squabbling. Martin is convinced he's good with his hands despite all the evidence to the contrary.' She stood. 'I must get the coffee.'

'I'm fine, thank you.'

Ruth ignored her and headed for the kitchen.

'What kind of a man was Shane?' Aoife asked.

Martin shrugged. 'I don't know. He was a good coach, that's why I chose him. But I'm a busy man. I should never have allowed myself to be talked into coaching, but rugby was a part of my life for so long that I was reluctant to give it up. It was fun at the beginning, but the strain of coaching and running my own business got too much. Shane was busy too. We did our jobs and went home. We didn't take the time to get to know each other.'

'Did you ever see him lose his temper?'

'No.'

'Did he ever appear depressed?'

'No, but remember I hadn't seen him for years before the murder.'

Ruth returned with a tray, which she placed on the table. She nodded at it for everyone to help themselves.

Aoife tasted the coffee she hadn't wanted. She had to admit Ruth's machine produced slightly better coffee than her Cuisinart, but it was also three times the size and probably ten times the cost. 'This is amazing.'

Ruth smiled. 'Thank you. It's the best coffee machine on the market. It only costs—'

'Ruth!'

'For heaven's sake, Martin. I was only saying—'

'Aoife didn't come here to discuss coffee. Now I have a very busy day ahead, so could we please get on with this?'

Ruth glared at him but she didn't reply.

'Tell me about Fiona. When did she join your book club?'

'About two years ago.'

'How did she find out about it?'

'Oh Lord!' Martin put his mug down with a bang. 'If we carry on at this pace, we'll be here for hours. Fiona was a full-time mother desperate for an opportunity to speak with people capable of intelligent conversation. There are millions of women like her all over the world, and I'd guess about half of them are in book clubs. They talk to other women and find out the good book clubs in the area.'

Aoife expected Ruth to be angry, but she nodded. 'That's true.'

'What was Fiona like?'

'She was a nice woman. I didn't always agree with her choice of books, but she was pleasant to everyone.'

'Did she ever seem upset or depressed?'

'No, not at all.'

'When was the last time you saw her?'

'Four days before the murder. We had book club in my house that week.'

'How did Fiona seem?'

'Her normal self.'

'Did she mention Shane or her family?'

'I don't think so. Certainly not to me, but I was hosting the event and I was in and out with coffee and food.' She smiled, and this time her eyes shone. 'Everyone loves when I host the book club. They all adore my coffee, and I've had so many compliments about my cakes.' She leaned forward as if to convey an important secret. 'The only way to have perfect baking every time is to—'

'Ruth! I don't have time for this.'

Ruth glared at him. 'Will you stop interrupt…' Her anger dissipated abruptly. 'Yes, you're right. I'm sure we're all very busy and I know you have to get to the office. Aoife, if we've answered your questions, we really must call this a day.'

Orla devoured a plate of spaghetti while Aoife described her morning.

'I loved that house. It was always such a happy place. It doesn't seem right that it's been stripped of all its colour.'

'It's not very happy now. It's as quiet as a church. About the only noise is Ruth and Martin bickering.'

'Did you find out anything useful?'

'No. Although I hadn't realised they'd known Shane for years. He and Martin coached the local rugby team.'

'Did they get on?'

'Martin claimed they hardly knew each other.'

'After four years? Is that likely?'

Aoife shook her head. 'I don't think so. What I can't understand is why Martin was there in the first place. He clearly didn't want to be. I'd only asked to speak to Ruth.'

'Moral support for his wife?'

'Why would she need moral support? And he wasn't very supportive. It was like I'd walked in on an argument. They sat as far away from each other as possible and snapped at each other the whole time.'

'Sounds like a lot of married couples to me.'

'Hmm. There was something off about their relationship. In one way Ruth was like a Stepford Wife. All she wanted to talk about was coffee and baking, but she wasn't in any way deferential.'

'Maybe Ruth's stuck at home all day and baking is her only pleasure.'

Aoife was silent for a few minutes. 'You know what it felt like? It was like Martin was there to run interference. And now I think of it, Ruth didn't answer all my questions because Martin kept interrupting.'

'You'll have to talk to her on her own.'

'It was hard enough getting her to speak to me once. I can't see her agreeing to it again.'

'You're meeting all the other members of the book club, aren't you?'

Aoife nodded.

'Somebody's got to know where Ruth hangs out. Wait until she's in a coffee shop or a restaurant and sit down beside her. Make her answer your questions.'

'What if she refuses?'

'I don't think she will. She met you once already and, you're right, it's obvious neither of them wanted to speak to you.'

'I bet she wouldn't have spoken to me at all if I wasn't a member of her book club.'

'Or maybe she couldn't ignore the fiancée of the detective investigating the death of a man she'd known for four years yet claimed was practically a stranger.'

'You think she and Martin are hiding something?'

Orla nodded. 'It certainly sounds like it.'

THIRTEEN

AOIFE HURRIED OFF to meet with the book club members. They all thought Fiona was nice. Two of them had been quite friendly with her. None of them knew Shane. The only interesting thing Aoife discovered was that Ruth and her sister had lunch every Saturday in Powerscourt.

Normally Amy loved spending time with her grandmother. Today she decided she had been treated very badly and was determined to make her displeasure clear. She refused to speak to Aoife the entire journey home. When they reached the house, she stormed into the kitchen and demanded ice cream. When Aoife refused, she dissolved into floods of tears. Twenty minutes later, she had another meltdown when Aoife wouldn't allow her to watch a movie. Aoife was worn out. Shouldn't Amy have grown out of the terrible twos by now? Was her behaviour Aoife's fault? Was she a terrible mother? There was no point in asking Conor. He hadn't even known he was a father when Blaine was Amy's age. She wished she could ask her mother for advice. She was beginning to feel quite weepy herself when Conor and Blaine arrived.

Aoife wiped her eyes and headed upstairs.

Conor found her in her bedroom. He wrapped his arms around her. 'What's wrong?'

Aoife sniffed. 'Nothing.'

'Tell me.'

'Amy's in a mood, I'm missing my mum and I haven't even started dinner yet.'

'Two of those I can help you with. Blaine!'

'Yeah?' Blaine called from the bottom of the stairs.

'There's a game of Snakes & Ladders in the TV cabinet. Can you keep Amy occupied while Aoife and I get dinner?'

Blaine went in search of Amy, and Conor led Aoife into the kitchen.

'You sit down and relax. I'll make dinner. What are we having?'

Aoife shook her head. 'I'll make it. You get the veg.'

From the sitting room, they could hear Amy's cries of 'I don't want to play a stupid game' followed by screeches of laughter as Blaine tickled her. Conor laughed. Aoife tried to smile, but Conor had his head in the fridge and didn't notice.

'Where are all the knives?' he asked.

Aoife looked at the knife block she kept on top of

the kitchen cupboards where Amy couldn't reach it. It was empty. Not again!

'I don't know. Ask Blaine.'

'How would Blaine know?' He turned to look at her. 'Tell me you're not still blaming Blaine for everything that goes missing around here?'

'Things only go missing while Blaine is in this house.'

'That's ridiculous, Aoife. Why would Blaine want your knives?'

'Why would he want my clothes, or my keys, or my wallet? He takes these things to annoy me, Conor.'

'No, Aoife. He doesn't. I'm sorry you've had a bad day but don't take it out on Blaine.' He opened the dishwasher. 'What are these?'

He pointed at the knives packed neatly into the cutlery tray.

Aoife slammed down the saucepan. 'I did not put those there. I would never leave knives in the dishwasher where Amy could find them, and I do not appreciate your son endangering my child.'

'Your child? What about my child, Aoife? I don't appreciate you blaming my son for your own carelessness.'

'So I'm careless now? I'm an irresponsible mother?'

'That's not what I said.'

'That's exactly what you said. Well, you can get your own dinner. Amy! We're going for a walk.'

Amy and Blaine appeared in the doorway. Aoife turned her head so she wouldn't have to look at him.

'I don't want to walk. I'm hungry.'

Aoife opened the cupboard, reached up to the top shelf and took down two bars of chocolate. 'Dinner,' she said, handing both bars to a delighted Amy and marching her out the door.

❧

Aoife took Amy to the park and then the supermarket. It was almost two hours later when they returned home. Conor's car wasn't in the driveway. Aoife's heart sank. Half of her had wanted Conor to be gone, but the other half had hoped he'd put his arms around her and everything would be okay.

'Where's Blainey?'

'They've gone home.'

'Why?'

'They weren't hungry.'

Aoife looked around the kitchen. Conor had made dinner and left two plates in the microwave. The kitchen was spotless.

❧

When Amy had eaten and gone to bed, Aoife phoned Orla.

'He's a good man, Orla. I do love him but I'm not sure we can get over this. I wouldn't be with a man who didn't like Amy.'

'Do you dislike Blaine?'

'Right now? Yes. I know I shouldn't say that, but it's true. I've been as nice as I can to Blaine, but he's deliberately causing trouble between Conor and me. I can't like some-one who would do that.'

'He's a teenager, Aoife. All teenagers are a pain. They don't think of anyone but themselves. In any case, Blaine isn't your problem. Conor is. You need to make him under-stand that Blaine is trying to break up your relationship. Then let Conor sort out Blaine. That's his job. Not yours.'

'Why couldn't I have met him before Katie got pregnant?'

'I don't think that would have helped.'

'Why not? You think he would have preferred Katie?'

'Well, as you were nine at the time, I certainly hope so.'

'You know what I mean.'

'Of course I know what you mean and it would defi-nitely be easier if neither of you had kids, but that would mean you wouldn't have Amy either.'

'Oh God! Why is everything so complic—'

'What?'

'He's phoning me. I'm not sure I want to tal—'

'Bye. Call me later.'

Aoife stared at her phone for a few seconds, then accepted the call.

'Hi.'

'Hi.'

'I left you dinner.'

'I saw that. Thank you.'

'Aoife, I don't want us to fight.'

'Neither do I.'

'You had a bad day and I should have been more

understanding. Can we just forget that stupid argument ever happened? Honestly, I wasn't calling you a bad mother. I think you're a great mother and you're very careful and responsible.'

'Thank you.'

'Blaine's great too.'

'I know.'

'Well, that's all that matters. Who cares about the rest of it? Do you want me to come around? Blaine's watching a movie. He won't mind staying here on his own.'

'No. I don't want you to miss out on your time with Blaine. I'll see you for dinner tomorrow. Okay?'

'Okay. I love you.'

'I love you too.'

Nothing was resolved, but at least they were still together. For now.

FOURTEEN

Lisa

LISA WOKE WHEN her mother touched her shoulder.

'Go to bed, Lisa. You're exhausted.'

Lisa struggled into a sitting position. 'I'm fine. Sorry, I'm not very good company, am I?'

'It's enough that you're here. You don't have to entertain me.' She handed Lisa a mug of tea and shuffled back to her seat.

'Mum, did you know Uncle Eamonn planned to leave half his business to Shane?'

'No. Who told you that?'

'Eamonn.'

'Did Shane know?'

'Yes.'

'Good. I'm glad. Eamonn was always a good man.'

'Which is more than could be said for his son.'

'I know you and Keith never got on, but you should try and put that behind you, Lisa. When Eamonn and I are gone, Keith will be your only family.'

'I think he might have murdered Shane.'

'What? That's ridiculous! Keith would never do something like that.'

'Wouldn't he? What if he had found out that he was losing half his inheritance to Shane?'

'He'd be angry, of course, but murder?' She stared into the distance.

'What?'

'I do remember Eamonn telling me there was a bit of trouble when Keith was younger.'

'What kind of trouble?'

'Keith was about fifteen at the time. He and a friend fell out over some girl they both liked. A group of them went swimming and some of the group claimed Keith had tried to drown the boy.'

'Oh my God!'

'It was probably an accident. Keith grabbed the boy's legs and pulled him under the water. Kids often do that to one another. Keith said he didn't mean any harm.'

'The friend didn't believe him?'

'The friend didn't remember the incident at all. It was others in the group who claimed Keith had deliberately tried to kill the boy.'

'Why didn't the friend remember?'

'Keith pulled the boy underwater and swam away.

He claims he didn't even know anything was wrong until others in the group jumped in to rescue his friend.'

'Why did he need rescuing?'

'Somehow the boy banged his head off a nearby rock. Eamonn always believed it was an accident. I never doubted it either until now.'

FIFTEEN

SATURDAY WAS ONE of those rare perfect weather days. There wasn't one cloud in the sky, something which, with the exception of the once-in-a-decade heatwaves, probably happened about twice a year in Ireland. It was warm enough not to have to wear a jumper but not so hot it was uncomfortable outdoors.

The restaurant in Powerscourt was always overcrowded on a Saturday. Aoife had arrived at midday in case Ruth and her sister were early diners. Almost two hours later, she had examined all the shops adjoining the restaurant and bought herself two rocky roads and six scones from the food shop. Every fifteen minutes she checked the restaurant. Just after 2 p.m. she spotted Ruth standing patiently at the end of the long self-service queue, talking to a much younger woman. Ruth's sister had the same tiny frame, but her brown curls reached her shoulders. Aoife picked up a tray and helped herself to a plate and knife before going out to the terrace.

In fine weather, everyone in Powerscourt tried to get a table on the terrace. The view of the gardens was spectacular. No matter what the season, the gardens were always a riot of colour, and the terraces, whose intricate designs were made up of tiny grey and white stones, were totally unique. Aoife wasn't a fan. Whenever she looked at them, she pictured the impoverished Irish peasants who, centuries earlier, had received a daily pittance to cart wheelbarrows of these stones the five miles from the beach in Bray. She preferred to look at the Sugarloaf Mountain. Its slightly off-centre peak really did resemble a mound of sugar that was about to topple over. Aoife admired it as she waited for Ruth to work her way to the top of the restaurant queue. A table on the terrace became empty, but Aoife stood back to allow the people behind her to take it. As Ruth was paying for her food, another table emptied. Aoife hurried over to claim it. She put the two scones she had bought on the plate. Piling most of the previous occupiers' plates and cups on her now empty tray, Aoife left them to one side for the waiters to remove. She kept one half-eaten salad, to give the impression she'd just finished a meal. As Ruth walked up and down the terrace, searching for an empty seat, Aoife bent down and rooted in her bag. Ruth asked if the seats were vacant and Aoife nodded vigorously, muttering 'Yes, yes' without raising her head.

Ruth and her sister placed their food on the table and continued a conversation about the dangers of sugar.

'It completely changed my eating habits, Susan,' Ruth said. 'I haven't been able to touch sugar since I watched the video.'

Susan laughed. 'Nothing on this earth could scare me off chocolate. If you told me it would take ten years off my life, I still wouldn't be able to give it up.'

'But that's exactly what it will do, Sus—' She stopped as Aoife raised her head from her bag and turned her attention to her scone.

'Aoife!'

'Oh, hi, Ruth. Nice to see you again.'

'Er, yes, of course. Er, lovely day, isn't it?'

'Beautiful.' Aoife smiled at Susan. 'Hi, we haven't met. I'm Aoife. I'm in Ruth's book club.'

'Susan. I'm Ruth's sister.'

'Yes, I can see that. You're very alike.'

Susan smiled. 'People always say that.'

'Susan, why don't we get a seat indoors? It's so hot out here.'

'Hot?' Susan stared at her sister. 'No, it isn't. You just said ten minutes ago that the weather was perfect. Is something wrong?'

'No, of course not. Tell me about the kids. How's Elena's new school?'

'Oh, she loves it. Elena's my youngest,' Susan explained. 'Do you have any kids, Aoife?'

'Yes, I have a three-year-old daughter.'

'That's such a great age. She's not with you today?'

'No, it's her weekend with her dad.'

'Oh! Well, I suppose it gives you a break. I'm always telling Ruth she should take advantage of the time her boys spend with their father. There have to be some advantages to divorce, right?'

Ruth glared at her. 'I'm sure Aoife doesn't want to hear about our kids, Susan.'

Susan frowned and was quiet for a moment. When nobody filled the silence, she said, 'How do you enjoy the book club, Aoife?'

'It's great, although we haven't had many meetings lately. I've enjoyed our WhatsApp chats, though.'

'Well, Ruth's is the very best book club in the area. She vets everyone who applies. Most of the members are librarians, teachers or college professors. They're all very serious about literature. To be honest, it's a little highbrow for me. I'm more of an Agatha Christie girl myself.'

Aoife smiled. 'Agatha Christie was a genius in her own right. She's certainly stood the test of time.'

'That she has.'

'And, of course, now that I'm single again, I have more time to devote to reading. How long have you been divorced, Ruth?'

Ruth twisted the thick gold bangle peeking out from beneath the cuff of her red silk blouse. 'Oh, I don't know if you could really call it a divorce. Martin and I are very close.'

Susan dropped her fork with a clatter. 'Please tell me you're not considering getting back together with that bastard. For God's sake, Ruth, hasn't he done enough damage to our family?'

'Susan! I do not want to discuss my marriage in public.' Ruth stood up. 'I need to get out of the sun.' She picked up her bag and marched into the restaurant.

Susan pushed back her chair. 'Excuse me, Aoife. I'll be back in a second.'

Aoife watched her follow Ruth into the restaurant. They stood inside the doorway and chatted for several minutes, casting furtive glances in Aoife's direction. Ruth walked away and Susan returned to the table. She picked up her bag, stretched her lips into something resembling a smile and said, 'Nice meeting you, Aoife.' Leaving her meal untouched on the table, she walked away without another word.

⊱

'Ruth and Martin are divorced?'

'And it wasn't a recent breakup either.'

'Did they actually say they were a couple?'

'How often do you go to someone's home and they say 'this is xxx' and by the way we're a couple?'

Orla laughed. 'So it was a simple misunderstanding?'

'No. They were deliberately giving the impression that they were together.'

'Why would they do that?'

'The only possible reason is that they thought it would make them seem less suspicious to the police.'

'But the police would have looked them up. They'd already know Martin and Ruth were divorced.'

'Yes, but if they had seen them together as I did, they'd assume they had reconciled.'

'Why would being together make them seem less suspicious to the police?'

'I interviewed five other members of the book club and asked them about Ruth. One of them knew about the divorce. She said Martin had been having affairs for years. Ruth turned a blind eye until she discovered one of his affairs was with her sister.'

'Susan?'

'No. The woman I spoke to couldn't remember the sister's name but she said it was something like Tricia or Triona.'

'So Martin had several women. Was one of them Fiona?'

'I don't know, but that's something he might prefer the police didn't find out.'

'True. But why would Ruth care if they found out?'

Aoife disconnected the call and sat staring at her notes. She had no idea how to find out what Ruth and Martin were up to, but she was pretty sure Derek could help.

⋖

Aoife had never been to Jenny and Derek's house before, and she was surprised to discover they owned a four-bed detached house directly across the road from Marley Park.

'This is a fabulous location, Jenny.'

'It should be for what we paid for it. Of course, it didn't help that we bought at the height of the property boom.'

She brought two cups of coffee into the sitting room and cleared a space on the cluttered table, shoving Trail-finders brochures and textbooks to one side.

'I set up a special room downstairs and the girls have a study area in their bedrooms, but they insist on sitting on the floor and using this table for their homework.'

'At least they're not refusing to study.'

'True. They're good kids.'

Aoife pointed at the travel brochures. 'Are you planning a holiday?'

'Yep. My fortieth birthday present from Derek. I told him we can't afford it, but he says he's been putting money away every month for ten years and we are going somewhere fabulous whether I want to or not.'

'Oh my God! I envy you.'

'You'll be going on your honeymoon soon. You should start planning now.'

'I don't think we'll go anywhere major. I intend to have a tiny wedding. I've done the whole big wedding once before and I didn't even like it the first time.'

'You didn't like the wedding? That's not a good sign.'

'It was a bad time. My parents weren't long dead. If I'd had any sense, I would have known that was the worst time to commit to anything. But then I was a teenager. Even if I'd had any family to warn me against it, I probably wouldn't have listened.'

'My parents didn't want me to marry Derek. I didn't

listen. I knew from day one that there was no other man for me.'

'How did you know?'

'Derek doesn't say much to most people. In the early days he didn't even say much to me, but I could see who he really was. I knew he was the kind of man who didn't give easily, but when he gave, he gave one hundred percent.' She smiled at Aoife. 'And I was right.'

'Actually, Derek is the reason I wanted to talk to you, Jenny. He doesn't trust me and he won't tell me anything about the investigation.'

'He—'

Aoife held up a hand. 'Don't get me wrong. I fully understand there are things Derek wouldn't be allowed to tell me, but he won't tell me anything at all. If I asked him the name of the victim, he'd say he couldn't share that information.'

Jenny laughed. 'Derek is a letter-of-the-law kind of guy. I don't see what I can do to help. I'm assuming you know I won't spy for you?'

'Of course I know. I was hoping you could tell me how I could win his trust.'

'In the short term, you can't. That would take years.'

'If you were me, what would you do?'

Jenny pointed at a plate of biscuits for Aoife to help herself, then sat back in her chair and sipped her coffee. 'Derek has two priorities in life—his family and bringing law-breakers to justice. He'd never break the law, but he'd bend it if it would help him catch Shane's murderer. Of course, first you'd have to convince him that Shane was actually murdered. Then you'd have to come up with evidence the police didn't have already. That would prove to him that you were valuable and worth collaborating with.'

'Even if I found that evidence, how would I know the police didn't already have it?'

'I'm not an investigator, Aoife. But I think if you find the kind of evidence that will impress Derek, you'll know it.'

SIXTEEN

THE FOCUS OF Aoife's interviews with the book club had changed. Clearly none of them knew Shane. Not many of them knew Ruth well, but most of them had at least one bit of gossip. Then she hit the mother lode—Bronagh.

Bronagh was one of those women determined to never show a trace of aging. Now in her late thirties, she didn't have a single wrinkle. She wore a white shirt, tied in a bow above a pancake-flat stomach and tight shorts that barely covered her behind. When she bent down to pick up a toy, the tendons in her leg stood out. She must spend half her days in the gym. Judging by the family photos that adorned every wall, Bronagh's children were still young. Aoife wondered if they would influence their mother's style choice once they became teenagers.

At the mention of Ruth, a shadow passed over her face.

'I set up the book club. It was supposed to be a joint venture.' Bronagh pursed her lips. 'But as usual, Ruth took over. Then she gets tired of it and just dumps us. Well, if she thinks I'm going to do all the work while she takes the credit, she has another thing coming.'

'You must have known Ruth a long time, then.'

'Oh yes, we used to be friends until she stabbed me in the back. I was the one who found our first sixteen members. Do you have any idea how hard it is to recruit serious readers for a book club that doesn't even exist?'

'It must have been difficult.'

'You have no idea. Then, when I had done all the work, she went on the radio and told everyone about her book club. She didn't even mention me. I was furious. And when I think of all the hours I wasted listening to her moaning about that useless husband of hers.'

'I heard they were divorced.'

'Aren't you lucky you only heard it? I lived through it. Every single day I listened to her moan. Martin this, Martin that. What would the kids do without their father? Would Martin be able to claim half her money?'

'Ruth has money?'

'You didn't know? She owns Kinsella Household Products. You must have heard of it. The company's very successful. It was doing well before the divorce, but it's worth even more now. I swear the only reason Ruth was interested in that book club was so she could sell her products to its members. We all dread going to her house.'

'Really? Ruth said everyone loves her coffee and her baking.'

'Her food's nice enough. It doesn't make up for the

constant sales spiel.' Adopting a high-pitched voice that bore no resemblance to Ruth's, Bronagh said, 'Have you ever tasted better coffee, ladies? Let me show you my new coffee machine. It's not even on the market yet, but I can put one aside for all of you. I'll even give you a special discount.' Bronagh snorted. 'There must be a hundred machines in that kitchen of hers, and she's bored us with minute descriptions of every single one. Thank God she only gets to host the book club twice a year or we'd have lost all our members by now.'

'I'd assumed the money was Martin's and Ruth was a stay-at-home mum. What does Martin do?'

'Different things. He had some business that went bankrupt and Ruth had to bail him out. When they divorced, he poured his settlement into a property company. Then the property market crashed and he lost everything. I used to think he deserved it. Now I think maybe he was due some compensation for putting up with Ruth all those years.'

Aoife was tiring of the bitching, and it was obvious Bronagh would happily rant about Ruth's perceived betrayal for hours.

'Did you know Shane and Fiona well?'

'Not really. I spoke to Fiona a few times. Shane didn't come to the book club very often, but it was obvious they were happily married. I told Ruth that, but of course she wouldn't listen to me.'

'After the murder, you mean?'

'What?'

'You told Ruth that Shane wouldn't murder his wife because they were happily married?'

'No. I told her to stop chasing after Shane.'

⁊

'Ruth was having an affair with Shane?'

'I don't know if it got that far, but she was always making up some excuse to have him around to her house.'

'Was this while she was married to Martin?'

'She definitely didn't have an affair with him while she was married. I'm sure of that. But she often talked about how great Shane was and how Fiona didn't deserve him. She told me she asked Shane around to give her advice about one of the salesmen she claimed to be having problems with. He came over several times after that. Of course, once she threw Martin out, Ruth didn't have to make up excuses any more. Shane felt so guilty he visited her two or three times a week to make sure she was alright.'

'Shane felt guilty about Ruth's divorce? Why?'

'He was the one who told Ruth about Martin's affair with Triona.'

'How did Shane know Martin was having an affair with Ruth's sister?'

'Martin and Shane used to be friends. I know because my husband and Martin went to school together. There's a gang of them used to play for the school rugby team. They meet up every rugby season and go to all the games. When they coached together, Shane used to go with them. He knew about Martin's affairs. We all did. Even Ruth. My husband knew about Triona but he didn't tell me. He was afraid I'd tell Ruth. I'm not sure I would have but, in any case, I didn't get the chance because Shane told her. Martin was furious. Ed—that's my husband—said he had to pull him off Shane. He said Martin would have killed him if he'd had the chance.'

SEVENTEEN

Lisa

'THEN IT WASN'T Keith after all?' Lisa's mother shut her eyes. 'Thank God! About the only thing that could make this worse is discovering my own family killed my son.'

'Aoife didn't say Keith was innocent. All she said was she had discovered another suspect.'

'Shane shouldn't have gotten involved in that man's marriage. If he'd minded his own business, they'd all be alive now.'

'You know what Shane was like, Mum. He got friendly with this woman and it was probably killing him watching her being treated so badly. Ruth's husband having an affair with her sister was probably the last straw.'

'And this woman—what's her name?'

'Ruth.'

'This Ruth liked Shane?'

'According to Aoife, Ruth thought Fiona didn't appreciate Shane. Presumably Ruth felt Shane would be happier with her.'

'Did this Ruth's husband know she liked Shane?'

'I don't know. Aoife's going to look into that.'

Lisa's mother nodded. 'Because if he thought Shane was going to get together with his wife, he'd believe Shane would get all the wife's money too.'

'True.'

'I don't know if that would cause anybody to murder an entire family, but it's certainly a motive for murdering Shane.'

EIGHTEEN

A VERY EXCITED Amy waved at Aoife as the car pulled away. Now that kindergarten was closed for the summer holidays, Conor and Blaine were including her in their activities at least once a week. Having to arrange their day around a three-year-old would put a damper on their plans. Aoife knew Conor was trying to give her the space to work on her investigation and she was very grateful.

Her gratitude dissipated when she returned to the house to discover her shoes had disappeared from the shoe rack in the hall. Blaine couldn't have taken them with him. Even if Conor hadn't noticed, Amy certainly would. Amy had been so excited she'd been glued to Blaine's side from the moment he entered the house. The only time he'd been alone was when he used the bathroom. A quick search of the bathroom and Aoife found her shoes in the clothes hamper. This was getting ridiculous. What could she do about it, though? Conor would never believe her and if she mentioned it, they'd fall out again.

She checked her watch. Time to leave. A quick Internet search and Aoife had discovered Martin owned a company called Martin's Way. It employed sixteen people and provided an 'elite service', focusing on property that was snapped up before it ever reached the local property websites.

Aoife arrived at Martin's office without an appointment. The office was off Stephen's Green. If the intention had been to design a reception area that was memorable and unique, it had been a huge success. The ceiling-to-floor-length windows overlooking the park were certainly impressive. The attempt to bring the park into the office, a little less so. Withering and overgrown plants were everywhere. An empty aquarium ran almost the length of one wall, and the white-tiled floor looked slightly grotty. At one end of the room was a large receptionist desk with four chairs. Only one was occupied. The girl behind the desk couldn't have been more than seventeen. She wore a black cropped T-shirt that displayed her belly ring. When a few seconds standing in front of her elicited no reaction, Aoife waved. The movement caught the girl's attention and she looked up from her mobile and removed her earplugs.

'Hi.' A tongue piercing caught the light as she spoke.

'Hi, I'm here to see Martin. I'm a friend of Ruth's.'

'Sure.' The girl picked up the phone and pressed a button, waited a few seconds and pressed another. 'This stupid machine is driving me crazy.' She came out from behind the reception desk and Aoife saw she was wearing ripped jeans and orange trainers. 'Come on,' she said, beckoning to Aoife.

They went down a long, wide corridor. The receptionist gave a perfunctory knock on the door and opened it. 'A friend of Ruth's,' she said, holding the door open to allow Aoife to enter.

'What?' Martin looked up from his computer, but the receptionist was gone. 'Aoife, what are you doing here? Why did she say you were a friend of Ruth's?'

'Oh, Ruth and I are old friends now. Didn't she tell you we had lunch together in Powerscourt a few days ago?'

'You and Ruth had lunch?'

'Yes, we had a great chat. I realised I'd completely misunderstood your relationship. Somehow I got the impression you were still married.'

'Really? I can't imagine how.'

'Neither can I, now that I've heard the whole saga about you and Ruth's sister.'

'Ruth told you about Triona?'

'I'm sorry. Was I not supposed to mention it?'

'Why are you here, Aoife?'

'Well, I realised I had forgotten to ask you some pertinent questions.'

'I really don't have time to talk to you today. Why don't you make an appointment with my receptionist on your way out?'

'Oh, there's no need for that,' Aoife said, taking a seat. 'I won't keep you long. What I wanted to ask you was this. Did it bother you that Shane and Ruth were in a relationship?'

'What relationship?'

'You didn't know?'

Martin was silent for a moment. Aoife watched as his neck turned a light red that spread to his cheeks. As the colour darkened, he burst out, 'That bastard! So that's why he told Ruth about my affair. I should have guessed. He'd known about my affairs for years and he'd never felt the need to mention them before. He was after Ruth's money, wasn't he?'

'When you're a rich woman, you never can trust the men around you.'

'If you knew how many times I've told Ruth that. She should have stuck with me. I married her when she had nothing. And if I hadn't helped her, she never would have built up that empire of hers. The woman had never set foot in an office in her life. I was the one who kept that business going until she could afford to hire staff. And what thanks do I get?'

'It must be hard trying to manage without money when you were used to it for so long.'

'You have no idea. I helped her choose that house and I suffered through the years of builders and architects just to find myself living in a two-bedroom apartment in the middle of nowhere. I told her it isn't a suitable place for the boys to visit but she doesn't care. She'd rather the boys were miserable than see me live with a modicum of comfort.'

'It doesn't bother her that your business is suffering either?'

'Not a bit. I used to employ sixteen staff. Now there's me and that moronic young one out there. If she wasn't on work experience, I wouldn't even have someone to answer the phone. Thank God I got Ruth to put the premises in my name years ago. At least I don't have to pay rent.'

'I can imagine! The rents around here must be extortionate.'

'When you deal with the wealthiest people in the country, you need impressive offices. Of course, now that cretin is in reception, I can only have clients here if they want out-of-office-hours appointments. Most of the time I take public transport to their homes or offices and pretend I came by cab. If anybody saw me in that bloody Fiesta, I'd be ruined.'

'And you never guessed that Shane and Ruth were an item?'

'She used to flirt with him, but that's Ruth's natural way of communicating with men. Except me, of course. Normally it doesn't mean anything.'

'Did Shane flirt with her?'

'Not that I noticed, but I suppose the bastard was too clever to give me any warning. If I'd known what he was up to, I might have been able to do something before he blabbed to Ruth about Triona.'

'How could you have stopped him?'

'I don't know. Smash his head in? Believe me, I wanted to.' He removed his glasses and rubbed his eyes. 'You know,

I've been a complete and utter idiot. When Ruth convinced me to pretend we were a happy couple, she said it was so I wouldn't come under suspicion. If the police saw we were reconciled, she said they would be less likely to believe I wanted revenge on Shane for breaking up our marriage. I was happy to go along with her plan. I thought it was a sign she still cared about me. Of course, now I can see her real aim was to protect herself. As that bastard's bit on the side, she'd be an immediate suspect.'

NINETEEN

AOIFE WENT STRAIGHT from her interview with Martin to Orla's office. Orla didn't have time to go to lunch, so she brought Aoife down to the company canteen. It was a lot more modern than any office Aoife had ever worked in. It was too early for lunch but, as she waited for Orla to get coffee, Aoife heard the manager explain the courses to the servers. It was like a posh restaurant except for the fact that it didn't deal in cash. Orla picked up a plate of cakes and swiped her ID card.

'So, Shane and Ruth were having an affair?' Orla said, tucking into an éclair.

'I don't know, the idea had obviously never occurred to Martin. But he definitely had an affair, and he definitely blamed Shane for his divorce. That gives him a motive for murder.'

'Mmm. Maybe. It might give him a motive to kill Shane, but why butcher Fiona and the kids?'

'Because Martin lost Ruth and the kids through the divorce, so he wanted Shane to feel the pain of losing his family too?'

'From what you said, I didn't get the impression that Martin was that bothered about the loss of his family. It's the loss of Ruth's money that's killing him.'

'He wouldn't be the first person to value money above people, and he wouldn't be the first to kill because he was denied money either.'

Aoife knew she wouldn't need to chase after Ruth. Ruth had her phone number. It was only a matter of time before she called. Aoife was still talking to Orla when her phone rang. 'Sorry,' she muttered to Orla as she took the call.

'Hi, Ruth.' She deliberately kept her voice light and airy.

'Why the hell did you tell my husband I was having an affair? How dare you! I never cheated on that lying scum. Not once.'

'Martin must have misunderstood me. I wondered if he suspected you and Shane of having an affair. I didn't say you actually had one.'

'What business is it of yours who I do or do not have an affair with? And why would you think Shane and I were an item anyway?'

'It came up during my investigation.'

Ruth took a second to reply, then said, 'That lying bitch, Bronagh. I give one interview to raise awareness of our book club and she holds a lifetime vendetta. There was nothing stopping her coming on the radio too. But could you blame me for not wanting her there? She dresses like she's in a competition to display as much of her body as possible. Who would look at her and think "intellectual willing to discuss serious literature"? Anyway, how was I supposed to know she expected me to mention her name every five seconds? Don't listen to that cow. Shane and I were friends. That's all.'

'But you wanted more.'

'Yes, I wanted more. And I'm sure I would have got more if…' Ruth's voice broke.

'You loved him, didn't you?'

'Of course I loved him. He was everything that husband of mine isn't. Kind, generous, faithful.' Her voice grew stronger. 'He stuck with that cow, Fiona, just because he'd been stupid enough to marry her. I know people think Shane was a monster, and I'm not defending what he did. Obviously he had some sort of a nervous breakdown. But the person who led him to that breakdown was that shrew.'

'Fiona?'

'Yes, Fiona. His bitch of a wife. She's the real reason that entire family is dead.'

TWENTY

'YOU'RE SAYING FIONA caused Shane to murder his family?'

'I know she did.'

'How do you know?'

'I saw the way she treated him. He was one in a million and she didn't appreciate him at all. Shortly after Martin and I separated, Fiona hosted the book club. I followed her into the kitchen and I overheard her saying to Shane, "How many times do I have to tell you to buy the coffee with the gold top, not the brown one? Nobody is going to drink this."'

'Was she shouting?'

'No. Well, she wouldn't in front of us, would she? But she wasn't hiding her contempt.'

'What did Shane say?'

'He said, "I think we have some of the old stuff left." You see what I'm saying? He was so used to being spoken to disrespectfully that it didn't even register with him that her behaviour was appalling.'

'If you disliked Fiona so much, why did you let her join the book club?'

'Shane asked me to. He was in the house one day when I got a phone call about the book club. He mentioned that Fiona was on the waiting list for two book clubs and could she join mine. I couldn't say no to him.'

'Were there other times when you felt Fiona treated Shane disrespectfully?'

'She told one of the girls in book club that she managed all their finances. According to Fiona'—Ruth sniffed— 'Shane was incapable of managing his own salary, so Fiona controlled all the expenditure. She treated him like a kid.'

'If there was nothing between you and Shane, why did you want me to think you and Martin were still together?'

Silence.

Had she hung up?

'Ruth?'

'I—I sent Shane some emails that were of a—*personal nature*. I'm sure the police have found them by now, and I figured they must be trying to work out who sent them. They're not the kind of emails you'd want strangers to see. What if they ended up in the papers and my friends, neighbours or, God forbid, my kids, saw them? I didn't want anybody guessing they were connected to me.'

'The police must know where the emails came from. They could easily trace the computer IP address.'

'I know, but I don't think they could connect the IP

address to me. I regularly have meetings with purchasing managers in hotels. The receptionists all know me. They don't mind me using the visitors' computer while I'm waiting.'

'Aren't those computers passworded?'

'Yes, but everybody is given the same password and they never bother to change them.'

'You don't think you were picked up on CCTV?'

'Maybe, but if anyone checked, I've been going in and out of most Dublin hotels fairly regularly for the last five years. And I only used the computers in the smaller hotels. The larger ones tend to have a business suite, and you need a room key to enter.'

'Why didn't you use your own computer?'

'I work from home. My computer is part of the company network. I don't know enough about IT to understand how that works, but I've heard of managing directors who were fired because the IT department caught them sending out porn. I didn't want anyone from my company reading the emails I sent Shane.'

'But you must have used a fake name too. Why did you do that?'

'If Fiona saw the emails, I didn't want her to be able to trace them back to me.'

'Did Shane know the emails were from you?'

Silence.

'Ruth, were you hoping Fiona would find them? Did you want Shane to deny knowing anything about them?'

Silence.

'Were you hoping if you planted enough evidence that Shane was having an affair, Fiona would throw him out?'

Aoife was about to speak again when Ruth said, 'Fiona didn't deserve Shane and he was too loyal to leave her. I thought if she left him, it would be best for everyone. And before you judge me, I was right, wasn't I? If they'd divorced, Shane could have found somebody worthy of him and that terrible tragedy would have been avoided.'

'What a psycho. If Shane hadn't died, I bet she'd have kept trying to break up their marriage for years.' Orla waved at a group of her colleagues who sat down at a nearby table. 'Or maybe Ruth got tired of sending emails that were having no effect. She might have decided the best way to end the marriage was to kill Shane's family.'

'Murdering his wife and kids wasn't likely to win Shane over. And the murderer killed Shane too, remember.'

'Well, Ruth took the risk that Shane would discover she was sending those emails. That was hardly likely to win Shane over either. Wasn't there a famous case in the US about a woman murdering her own children because her lover didn't like kids? Is it so much of a stretch to think Ruth would murder another woman's kids so she could have their father all to herself?'

'It doesn't seem very likely, and if the object was to have Shane to herself, why kill him too?'

'Maybe he returned home unexpectedly before she had

time to escape. He was furious, she was angry he didn't appreciate what she had done for him, so she killed him.'

'The police say he cut his own wrists.'

'Okay. Maybe he was so distraught at the sight of his dead family that he didn't want to live anymore, so he cut his wrists before Ruth could stop him.'

'That's not very likely either. If you discovered your family murdered, wouldn't your first reaction be shock? I imagine it would take a while for depression to set in.'

'I've no idea.' Orla finished one éclair and reached for a second.

'How do you stay so thin?'

'Good genes. Mum says she could eat anything until she turned thirty. She's been dieting ever since. I figure I have another six years of eating whatever I like and I intend to enjoy them.' She cut the éclair into thin slices and offered the plate to Aoife, who declined.

'You know, Aoife, maybe you were right about Shane having gambling problems. His own wife said he was incapable of managing their finances. If Ruth didn't kill him, maybe the murders were revenge for unpaid debts after all.'

'Yeah, that's the next thing I plan to look into.'

Shane's finances weren't the only thing Aoife needed to figure out. On the journey home, she decided if she couldn't talk to Conor about Blaine's behaviour, she would have to deal with Blaine directly.

Her opportunity came that evening, when they ran out

of milk and Conor offered to get some. Aoife ran upstairs and left her iPad in Amy's room. Three deep breaths and she headed downstairs.

'Amy, would you like to watch a movie for an hour before dinner?'

Amy's mouth dropped open.

'Just this once, as a special treat.'

'Yes, please.'

'I left the iPad on your bed.'

Amy raced upstairs. Aoife sat opposite Blaine, who was playing a game on his phone. 'Blaine, we need to talk.'

Blaine's thumbs clicked away at the keyboard, but he raised his eyes to meet hers.

'We can't go on like this. I understand why you don't want somebody else in your dad's life, but is that fair to him? You have your mum and stepdad in London. Do you want your dad to be all alone?'

Blaine shrugged.

'Please talk to me, Blaine. I know you love your dad. You want him to be happy, don't you? That's what I want too.'

'You don't give a damn about my dad.'

'Blaine! Of course I love your dad. Why would you say that?'

Blaine's eyes returned to his screen. 'I know you don't give a damn about him. He told Mum he asked you to marry him but you said no. You're just screwing with him until you're bored.'

'That is not true, Blaine.' When he refused to look at

her, Aoife knelt on the floor beside him, put her hands on his shoulders and looked into his eyes. 'I love your dad more than anybody in the world, except Amy.'

Blaine shrugged off her hands. 'Liar!'

'I am not—'

'What's going on here?' Conor stood in the doorway.

Aoife got to her feet. 'Blaine and I were discussing our differences.'

'Blaine, why did you call Aoife a liar?'

Blaine was silent. Conor waited, arms crossed. Finally, Blaine snapped, 'Because she is a liar. She doesn't love you. You told Mum she won't marry you. Instead of going on holidays like we always do, I'm stuck here in this stupid house because you want to spend time with someone who doesn't give a damn about you.'

'I didn't say Aoife wouldn't marry me. I said she won't get engaged. And we are not spending time in this house because I want to be with Aoife. We're here because you, I, Aoife and Amy are going to be a family soon and you need time to get to know each other.'

'I don't want to get to know her. And you will never be part of her family, Dad. Jason and Amy are her family. Jason loves her too. Can't you see that?'

'Second marriages are complicated, Blaine. I still love your mum, but I love Aoife in a completely different way.'

'You don't understand anything!' Blaine ran out of the room. A few seconds later the front door banged and they watched him tramp across the fields, sending the startled sheep scattering in all directions.

'Shouldn't you go after him?'

Conor shook his head. 'There's no point talking to him now. I'll wait until he's calmed down.'

He followed her into the kitchen and switched on the kettle.

'Aoife, why won't you get engaged?'

'Oh, Conor, not that again. I've told you; I'll marry you the very day my divorce comes through, but I don't want a formal engagement.'

'So you said, but you haven't explained why. Now Blaine thinks you don't want to get married. How am I going to get him to take us seriously if you refuse to commit to our relationship?'

'Is that what you think? That I'm refusing to commit?'

'I don't know what to think. I believe you love me, but maybe you're afraid to get married again. Is that it? Do you want to wait a few years before remarrying?'

'Would you be okay with that?'

Conor stiffened. He took two mugs from the shelf and placed them beside the boiling kettle. With his back to Aoife he said, 'So I'm right? You don't want to get married for another few years?'

'No! That's not what I said. Conor, look at me.'

When he turned, Aoife said, 'I love you. I want to spend every minute of the rest of my life with you, and I promise you, I do not want to delay our marriage. I will marry you the very first day it is legal for us to do so.'

'But you won't get engaged?'

'No.'

Conor finished making the coffee. He handed her one and said, 'Why?'

'Why do we need to be engaged? Don't you believe I love you?'

'I believe you try to distract me or change the subject every time I mention getting engaged. If there's a problem, why not tell me about it?'

'Because it has nothing to do with you and I don't want you involved.'

'Involved in what?'

'Involved in what remains of my relationship with Jason.'

'Do you still have feelings for him?'

Aoife snorted. 'Oh, I have lots of feelings for him. Few, if any, are positive.'

'Then what's the problem?'

'Blaine was right about one thing. Jason still loves me, or at least he thinks of it as love. He's got used to you being in my life, but if he even heard a rumour we were engaged, he'd go off his head.'

'It's only natural that he'd be upset, Aoife. He'll learn to accept it in time.'

'No, Conor. He won't. He'll make all our lives a misery. Even Amy's. I'm sure he'd try to turn her against you.'

'He'd do that to a little girl?'

'I'd bet on it.'

'But surely he'll react the same way to us getting married? Wouldn't it be best to get engaged first so he could get used to the idea?'

'No, it wouldn't. In Jason's mind, marriage equals ownership. That's why he pushed me into marrying him when we were still teenagers. Although we're no longer together, I'm still Jason's wife, therefore he still owns me. When our divorce comes through, I'll be without an owner, but in Jason's head, he has special status as my previous owner.'

'You're not serious?'

'I'm deadly serious. You see, this is why I didn't want to tell you. Nobody understands what he's like.'

'I didn't say I didn't believe you.'

'No. But I can see that you don't. My relationship with you is something Jason detests, but it doesn't threaten his status as my owner. In Jason's mind, an engagement would be my signal that I intend to change ownership. If he allows that, then he will have no special claim to me. Jason will do anything to prevent that. The closer it got to zero hour, the more desperate he would become. Once we're married, his special status will be destroyed. I'm hoping he'll lose interest in me and move on.'

'You don't think there's any possibility you might be overreacting?'

'None at all. You don't know Jason. I know him far too well. If we get engaged, he will freak out. He'll use anybody and everybody to split us up, and he knows his strongest weapon against me is Amy.'

When Blaine hadn't returned an hour later, Conor went looking for him. He texted Aoife that he had found Blaine in the local shop and they were on their way home. Now that Conor had witnessed Blaine's hostility towards her, Aoife wondered if he would be more prepared to believe Blaine was harassing her. There was no point worrying about it now. Tomorrow was going to be a big day. Jenny had told her what she needed to do to convince Derek to collaborate with her. She'd finally got the evidence she needed.

TWENTY-ONE

'HI, DEREK, IT'S Aoife.'

'What can I do for you today, Aoife?'

'I know you don't want me investigating the Grogan case. You think I'll get in the way. But what if I could prove you wrong?'

'How could you do that?'

'What if I had information that would be of value to you?'

'Withholding information is a crime, Aoife. If you know something, tell me about it right now.'

'What I know is one person's unsubstantiated report of what happened. That makes it hearsay. I don't believe there is any law that requires me to report hearsay.'

'What makes you think I would be interested in this gossip?'

'I understand you may be trying to trace some emails. Is that right?'

When it became obvious Derek didn't intend to reply, Aoife said, 'I've heard rumours that Shane was receiving emails of a personal nature. If that's true, then you must be trying to trace the person who sent them. I have an idea who it might be. Is this information that might be of interest to you?'

'I'm not working today and Jenny's gone out. I can't leave the girls alone while Caoimhe's boyfriend is here. I'd rather not become a grandfather quite yet. Can you call to the house?'

Derek answered the door and showed her into a small room that had been converted into an office. Aoife wondered if the room was always this sparse or if he had cleared every surface for her visit.

'If you know about the emails Grogan received, then any information you have is vital to the investigation. I can't stress strongly enough how important it is that you tell me everything you know, Aoife. This is a criminal investigation. You don't get to decide what parts of the investigation are relevant. Withholding evidence of any kind is a criminal offence. Think what it would do to Detective Inspector Moloney's career if you were arrested.'

Aoife felt a momentary pang of guilt, but she stuck to her guns. 'It's just one person's story at this stage, Derek. The point I'm trying to make is that I could be very useful to you. People will tell me things they wouldn't tell the police. We could be a team. Isn't that in everyone's interest?'

Derek sat back in his chair. He stared into space for a few minutes, then said, 'What do you want to know?'

✎

'Did Shane have a gambling problem?'

'If I answer that question, will you tell me who sent those emails to Grogan?'

'Yes.'

'Very well, as Detective Inspector Moloney's future wife, I'll take your word on that. We have looked into Grogan's finances and we can account for all but a few euros of his income. He bought most things by credit card.'

'There was no sign that he was spending more money than he earned?'

'None at all.'

'That's not very much help, Derek. Can you tell me anything that would be of benefit to me?'

'That wasn't our agreement.'

'Come on, Derek. I'm trusting you to act in good faith. I'm going to help you. Give me something in return.'

Derek looked at her for a long time. Then he said, 'Grogan isn't the one with the gambling problem.'

'Who is?'

'His cousin, Keith.'

✎

'Keith has a gambling problem? How do you know that?'

'We found a text from Grogan. Keith's father had mentioned how pleased he was that Grogan and Keith were on friendlier terms. He'd noticed Shane's name on Keith's expenses forms. Shane said in his text that he didn't know what Keith was playing at, but he wanted no part in Keith fiddling his expenses. When we looked into it, we found Keith is heavily in debt and recently remortgaged his home.'

'Do you think he was stealing from his father's company and Shane found out?'

'From what we can tell, the company is doing quite well. Preliminary enquiries have indicated that Keith has no involvement in its financial affairs. I think fiddling his expenses is the limit of his fraudulent activity.'

'Right now, maybe. But if Keith gets further into debt, I'm sure he'll talk his father into giving him more control. Can I tell him what Keith is up to?'

'Absolutely not. That information was given to you in confidence.'

'I won't say anything without your approval, but I think somebody should tell Keith's father. We can't just stand by and let his son ruin his life's work. And what about Keith's wife and kids? Does his wife know he remortgaged the house?'

'Her signature is on the agreement.'

'Is it really her signature or did Keith forge it? And even if it is her signature, I bet she has no idea why he needs the money.'

'That's their business and nothing to do with either of us.'

'Derek, you said you want to help families. Help Keith's

by letting me tell his father about his gambling problem. I won't mention how I found out. If he doesn't believe me, then at least I tried.'

Derek shut his eyes and massaged his temples. After a few moments, he looked at her. 'I shouldn't be doing this, but alright. Provided there's no mention of me or the police.'

⁓

Aoife kept her part of the bargain with Derek and repeated her conversation with Ruth. Derek listened in silence. With what was clearly an immense effort, he kept his voice even as he said, 'That is not hearsay, Aoife. That is a confession.'

'I can't be sure Ruth is telling the truth.'

'As you very well know, this information incriminates Ruth, and it should have been brought to my attention immediately.'

'I am bringing it to your attention immediately.'

'You are using it as a bargaining tool to get your own way. Detective Inspector Moloney is very respected in our profession. He deserves a wife with the highest morals.'

'Excuse me! Are you saying—'

'I am saying that journalists are required to have a certain amount of moral flexibility. It's a luxury that is not allowed to senior policemen or to their wives.'

'Derek, I—I really don't know what to say. The last thing I want is to argue with you. Your wife is my friend and you work with Conor, but you have absolutely no right to speak to me like that.'

'I am only speaking the truth.'

'And I suppose the police never mislead peop—never mind. I'm leaving.'

Aoife was fuming as she drove home. How dare he! She could write a book on all the immoral things the police had done. Hell, she could fill an entire library. And to question her morals when he had just admitted he shouldn't be giving her information about Keith. The hypocrisy!

Aoife was so enraged it was several hours before she remembered what she had discovered about Keith. The conversation with Keith's father was long and difficult. He was alternately angry, shocked and incredulous. Aoife ended the conversation with 'I know this must be difficult to hear, and I understand you can't take my word for it, especially when I'm unable to tell you how I found out. You can conduct your own investigation or not as you please. What you do with the information is entirely up to you.' She hung up before he could reply.

'Are you still angry with Blaine?' Conor asked when they got a few moments to themselves after dinner. 'I've never seen you this furious. Smoke is practically coming out of the top of your head.'

'No, Blaine's a kid and he believed what he said was the truth. The person who annoyed me is a full-grown adult.'

Conor grinned. 'Want me to sort them out for you?'

Aoife laughed and her bad humour evaporated. She even smiled at Blaine when he entered the room. He ignored her.

⌇

Aoife was at work the following morning when her phone buzzed. She checked the caller ID: Jenny. Her finger hovered over the screen for a few moments, then she accepted the call.

'Hi, Jenny. I take it Derek told you about our argument.'

'You and Derek had an argument? Why?'

'Basically, he told me I was immoral and not a suitable wife for Conor.'

Jenny was silent for so long that Aoife checked her screen to make sure they hadn't been disconnected.

'Tell me what happened, Aoife.'

⌇

When Aoife repeated her conversation with Derek, Jenny groaned.

'Oh God! I'm sorry, Aoife. Derek shouldn't have spoken to you like that. He's a good man, but everybody has their faults. Derek's is his inability to see shades of grey. To him, things are either right or wrong. I'll talk to him.'

'No, Jenny. Don't. It's not your problem. You and I are still friends. You don't need to get involved in this.'

'I have to get involved, Aoife. Derek obviously upset you, and he was upset too. I could tell something was wrong with him yesterday, but he claimed it was work.

You're both good people and you're both important to me, so let me sort this out, please.'

'Okay. I better get back to work.'

'Bye.'

Her hands had barely touched the keyboard when Jenny phoned again.

'I forgot to tell you why I rang. Ruth's dead. She was murdered.'

TWENTY-TWO

'RUTH WAS MURDERED? When?'

'Sometime during the night. She had been at some corporate event and got home shortly after midnight. The last person to see her alive was the babysitter. The housekeeper found her dead body this morning.'

'How was she killed?'

'Her throat was cut.'

Conor phoned Aoife that afternoon. He wouldn't be able to come around for dinner. He had been called into work urgently. It annoyed Aoife that he didn't say why he was working. She hadn't mentioned her meeting with Ruth, but Conor knew they were in the same book club. Didn't he trust her? Derek had obviously mentioned it to Jenny.

That evening, when she and Amy were in the house on their own for the first time in weeks, Derek phoned.

'I owe you an apology, Aoife.'

He didn't sound apologetic. She thought she detected an undercurrent of resentment, but mostly he sounded bored. Aoife didn't care. She had much bigger fish to fry.

'Thank you. Are you investigating Ruth's murder?'

'No. That tragedy has raised new questions about the Grogan case. I will be working on those. Detective Inspector Moloney will oversee the investigation into Ruth's murder.'

'Did you speak to Ruth yesterday?'

'Yes. I called to her house in the afternoon. She said she wouldn't speak to me without getting legal advice. We agreed that she would be in my office at eleven this morning. We were informed of her murder at eight-thirty when her housekeeper found her in the kitchen.'

'You think it was the same person who killed the Grogans?'

'I think it's a good thing her children were with their father last night.'

'Oh my God! You're right. The entire family could have been wiped out. Those poor boys. I wonder what will happen to them now.'

'They'll live with their father, I presume. He's not going to risk their fortune falling into anybody else's hands.'

'I didn't think of that. The boys inherited everything?'

'Yes, as soon as they're of age.'

'What age are they now?'

'Ten and six.'

❧

When Derek hung up, Aoife phoned Orla.

'What's all that noise? Are you in a bar?'

'A restaurant. We're going to a club later. Who did you say was killed?'

'Ruth, the woman who started the book club.'

'And her throat was cut?'

'Yes. Orla, I think it might be my fault.'

'What's your fault?'

'I told Martin that Ruth had an affair, and a few days later she's murdered. It can't be a coincidence, can it?'

'Hang on a sec, I'm going outside.'

The background noise became muted, then disappeared.

'Okay, so Martin believes his wife had an affair years ago. Why would that cause him to cut her throat?'

'Maybe that's what he does when he loses control. He killed the Grogans because Shane broke up his marriage, and he killed Ruth because she cheated on him.'

'I don't know, Aoife.'

'They knew each other, Orla. They died in exactly the same way. How likely is it that they were killed by two different people?'

'Not likely, that's true. Their murders must be connected, but the connection may not be Ruth and Martin's marriage.'

'What else could it be?'

'All three were members of the same book club.'

✒

'You think somebody is cutting the throat of people who belong to my book club?'

'It's as good a motive as any.'

'But it makes no sense.'

'That's precisely my point. Everyone is trying to find reasonable explanations why Shane murdered his family or why somebody else murdered Shane, but nobody is ever going to come up with one. Whoever the murderer is, he's obviously not capable of rational thought. Killing members of a book club probably makes as much sense to him as anything else.'

TWENTY-THREE

Lisa

'BUT THAT MEANS the police have accepted that Shane didn't murder anyone. Doesn't it?'

'I don't know, Mum. All Aoife said was that the police now feel there are additional questions that have to be answered.'

'Thank God. Oh Lisa, thank God. People will know Shane didn't murder his family now. Won't they?'

'I hope so. But there are some who will still point out that Shane had no defensive wounds and that the note pinned to the door was in his handwriting.'

'It's a start, love. They're going in the right direction at last.'

'I told Aoife I'd help her. She can't investigate two murders, hold down a part-time job and look after a toddler at the same time. She's going to get me a list of everyone Ruth contacted in her last two weeks and I'll check them out.'

'That's good, Lisa. I'll help. It will be a relief to finally be able to do something to clear Shane's name.'

TWENTY-FOUR

AOIFE WAITED A week before visiting Martin's office. Her plan was to offer her condolences and get some indication of Martin's reaction to the murder. She hoped Martin would be so devastated she would be left in no doubt of his innocence.

Aoife blinked as she entered the reception area. It was a hive of activity. Every seat was occupied. The tables were covered in glossy brochures, the plants had all been replaced and several new ones added. The aquarium was fully stocked, the white-tiled floor shone and the walls had been repainted. A lot of money had been spent in the few weeks since her last visit. There was no sign of the young girl with the belly ring. In her place were three receptionists clicking away on keyboards.

A pretty, highly groomed young woman in a navy suit hurried to greet Aoife.

'Good afternoon, I'm Charlotte. May I help you?'

'I'm here to see Martin.'

'Do you have an appointment?'

'No, but could you tell him Aoife is here and I'm happy to wait until he's free.'

'Yes, of course. Please take a seat. Would you like tea or coffee?'

'Coffee, please.'

'Would you prefer a latte, cappuccino or espresso?'

She took Aoife's order and headed for the coffee machine, muttering into her headset. 'Aoife here to see Martin. She doesn't have an appointment but she's happy to wait.'

Charlotte returned a few minutes later with a small tray containing a cappuccino in a china mug, and a matching china plate with three biscuits. 'Martin is unable to see you today, I'm afraid. He suggested you ring his secretary and make an appointment.' She put a business card on the tray. 'This is Isabella's number. Please take your time and enjoy your coffee. We look forward to welcoming you again to Martin's Way.'

She rushed off to greet an elderly couple who had just entered.

Aoife glanced at the card. There was no point phoning Isabella. Martin obviously would not agree to meet her. She picked up her coffee and sipped it slowly. It was twelve-twenty. With his newfound wealth, she was willing to bet Martin wouldn't eat lunch in his office. If she approached him in a packed reception area, it would be difficult for him to ignore her.

She took out her phone.

'Hi, Jenny. I need a list of Ruth's recent phone calls. I presume the police have it. I can't ask Conor or Derek to get it for me. Any idea how I could get my hands on it?'

'Oh God, Aoife, you'll get us all strung up. Okay, I'm only telling you this because Derek was so horrible to you. There's a guy in the department called Frank O'Meara. His wife got drunk at last year's Christmas party and said something that gave her friends the impression that Frank sells information to the press. I heard the story third-hand and I've no idea if it's true, but you could give it a go.'

'Thanks, Jenny.'

'Actually, on second thought, don't talk to Frank yourself. You don't want anybody getting the idea Conor is involved. Get Lisa to speak to him.'

Aoife finished her coffee and gestured to Charlotte. 'Would it be possible for me to have a second coffee? I've walked so much this morning, I'm exhausted.'

Charlotte looked slightly concerned but assured her it was no problem. As she was returning with the coffee, a woman in her mid-thirties entered. She was medium height, slender with very short blonde hair. Something about her face was familiar.

'Hi, Charlotte, is he alone?'

'Good afternoon, Triona. His meeting should end in the next ten minutes.'

Triona? Ruth's sister Triona? She was taller than her

sisters, the blonde hair was probably highlights, but there was something about her that reminded Aoife of Ruth. The eyes, maybe?

'I'll go up. See you later.'

Triona waved at Charlotte as she headed for the lift. Charlotte handed Aoife the coffee.

'Thank you. Have you worked here long, Charlotte?'

'It's my first week.'

'You're obviously very good at your job. I've noticed several of the clients greet you by name. The lady you were just talking to, for instance.'

Charlotte smiled. 'Oh, Triona is here every day. I know her well by now. Excuse me.' She hurried off to greet another client.

Aoife sipped her coffee. She angled her chair so she would have a better view of the lift. Every few minutes the doors opened and the lift emptied. After about ten minutes she saw them. As the lift door opened, Martin and Triona drew apart. There were several inches between them as they strode out of the office. Aoife gathered up her things and followed them. When they rounded the corner, Martin put his arm around Triona and she lifted her face for a kiss. They got into a brand-new Mercedes and drove away.

TWENTY-FIVE

Lisa

LISA SAT AT a table near the door and watched everyone who entered the bar.

Twenty minutes later, exactly on schedule, Frank O'Meara entered. He took a seat at the bar and chatted to the barman. When another customer caught the barman's attention, Lisa sat on the empty barstool beside Frank.

'Hi.' She smiled at him.

'Hi.' Frank looked away. He obviously wasn't in the mood to flirt with strange women.

'Bad day at work?' she asked.

'You could say that.'

'Me too. My boss told me to get my hands on a list of phone calls the police have, but I have no idea how to get it.'

She had his attention now.

'Who do you work for?'

'*The Sun.*'

'What list are you looking for?'

'Calls Ruth Kinsella made a few days before she died.'

'Tough one, that. Keep an eye on my beer. I'll be back in a minute.'

Twenty-five minutes later he returned carrying a small manila envelope.

'Usual terms?'

Lisa had no idea what that meant. She took out four hundred euros and left it in front of her.

'Are you serious? My terms are one thousand euros. They always have been and they always will be.' He put a hand on the envelope and drew it closer to him.

Frank was obviously a chancer. A chancer would expect to bargain, wouldn't he?

'Okay, five hundred. That's our agreement and you know it.'

Without another word, Frank slid the money into his pocket and, leaving the manila envelope on the counter, strolled out of the bar.

∽

'I got it, Mum.'

'I was so worried. I had visions of the police arresting you. What happened?'

'It was child's play. He was in the bar at the exact time, just like Aoife said he would be.'

'How much did he charge?'

'Five hundred. He wanted a thousand, but I talked him down.'

'If we find something that clears Shane, it was well worth it.' She reached for her glasses. 'Let's start on it now. I'll call out the names and you ring them.'

Lisa took out her phone and checked to see her number was still withheld. 'Right. Start with the last number and we'll work our way back.'

'What excuse are you going to make for phoning these people?'

'It depends on who they are. If I recognise the name, I'll hang up. Otherwise, I'll say I'm Ruth's secretary, that I'm going through a list of calls Ruth made before she died to ascertain if there are any outstanding issues we should be dealing with and could they tell me what their call was in connection with.'

'Where do you come up with these ideas, Lisa?'

Lisa grinned. 'An overactive imagination.'

She dialled the last number Ruth had phoned. A boy answered, presumably Ruth's son. The call before that went to voicemail. It was Ruth's sister. Then there was a Pizza Hut, one of the members of the book club, Ruth's parents and a hairdresser.

'This could take a while, Mum. I'll make us a cup of tea to keep us going.'

TWENTY-SIX

AOIFE SEARCHED THE Internet until she found a picture of Ruth's sister. Yes, it was the same Triona. Aoife had assumed Triona would be the younger sister, but she was at least five years older than Susan, much closer to Ruth's age.

'Jenny, it's Aoife again. I have a question for Derek. Could you ask him if the police are aware that Martin and Ruth's sister Triona are still a couple?'

'I'll get back to you in a few minutes.'

Six minutes later the phone rang.

'Derek said Triona and Martin never completely broke up. They stopped meeting in public, but when Martin's neighbours were questioned, they said Triona has been a regular at Martin's house for several years now.'

TWENTY-SEVEN

Lisa

LISA'S MOTHER PUT the list on the table and removed her glasses.

'This is the last one, Lisa.'

'Are you tired, Mum? Do you want to take a break?'

'No, we're nearly there. Let's get it finished.'

Lisa dialled the number and a young girl answered.

'Hi.'

'Hi. Who am I speaking to?'

'Natasha. Who's this?'

'Hi, Natasha, I'm Anna, Ruth Kinsella's secretary. I'm going through her paperwork and I see she phoned you the day she died. Would you mind if I asked what that was in connection with?'

'Anna? What happened to Dee?'

'Dee?'

'Ruth's secretary. Don't tell me she got rid of Dee too?'

Lisa could have kicked herself. Idiot! Why hadn't she taken the time to find out the name of Ruth's real secretary?

'I don't know. I've only been working here a few days. Nobody's mentioned Dee to me.'

'That bitch! She treated poor Dee like a slave for eight years and then she just gets rid of her. Did she have a nanny cam watching her too?'

'Nanny cam?'

'That's how the bitch got rid of me. She filmed me on the sofa with my boyfriend. It was 11 p.m. and the kids were in bed. What did she expect me to do? Stand guard outside their bedroom doors?'

'You were Ruth's nanny?'

'Oh, didn't I say that?'

'Why did Ruth phone you if she had already fired you?'

'That's how she fired me. She didn't even have the decency to tell me in person.'

'And she had a nanny cam watching you?'

'Can you believe it? It wasn't even the legal type. I googled it and it's not against the law if it doesn't record audio, but Ruth's did. It was voyeuristic. I've seen porn that was less explicit.'

'You saw the video?'

'Ruth showed it to me.'

'I thought you said Ruth fired you by phone. When did she show you the video?'

'Oh, alright, she didn't show it to me. Don't tell anyone I said that, okay?'

'Okay, but how did you get to see the video?'

'I heard what happened to Ruth, obviously. I knew the police would go through the house for evidence. I live nearby, so it wasn't hard to keep an eye on it. As soon as the police moved out, I used my key and let myself in. It was such a relief the police hadn't found it.'

'How did you know where to look?'

'I googled the different types of nanny cams. There's one that's hidden in an air freshener. I knew the minute I saw it. Ruth had air fresheners all over the place.'

'Where's the air freshener now?'

'They're still in the house. I only took the memory cards.'

'How many were there?'

'There were two in the basement and one in the play-room, sitting room and the kid's bedrooms. Six altogether.'

'What did you do with them?'

'Nothing yet. I was going to destroy them, but my boyfriend wants to watch the one we're in.'

'But Ruth was murdered while they were in the house. They're evidence, Natasha.'

'Oh no, I flicked through them and the only people they recorded are Ruth, me, the kids and the babysitter she hired while she was between nannies.'

'Natasha, my husband is a law student and I help him revise sometimes. I'm pretty sure keeping that information from the police is a criminal offence.'

'Really? But the murderer isn't on the recordings. I've checked.'

'It's still withholding evidence.'

'Oh God! I'll get rid of them right now.'

'You can't do that, Natasha. If the police learned they existed, you'd be charged with destroying evidence. That's an even more serious crime.'

'How would they ever find out?'

'There's always a trail. A credit card receipt, a friend she discussed nanny cams with, something like that.'

'What am I going to do? I can't have an entire police station watching us. I just can't.'

'If you like, I have a friend whose fiancée is a detective. I can give it to him. That way you could be sure the recording isn't doing the rounds of the police station.'

Lisa spent the evening listening to the recordings. She skipped over Natasha and her boyfriend, but otherwise she watched every single minute. About eighty percent of it was kids playing, fighting or eating. One recording consisted of the babysitter watching a movie. Lisa worked on the list of calls Ruth made while she waited. Opposite Natasha's name, she typed, 'Nanny/could be something there. Looking into it. Phone me.' She saved the list and emailed it to Aoife.

The movie the babysitter was enjoying was a particularly boring one, and Lisa was relieved when Ruth returned halfway through and the babysitter left. Once she was alone, Ruth switched off the TV and tidied the room. She was fluffing cushions when she froze. Had she heard something? She waited a few seconds, then, phone in hand, went into the hall. What happened next wasn't caught by any camera, but Lisa clearly heard a deep voice growl, 'You move, you die.'

∼

'What are you going to do?'

'I can't keep it, Mum. It's evidence.'

'Give it to Aoife. She can take it to her detective.'

'I can't. We agreed she would never discuss the case with Detective Moloney.'

'Phone him yourself, then.' She checked her watch. 'Heavens, look at the time! No wonder I'm hungry.'

'I'll make dinner in a minute.'

'It's okay. I'll get it started. You sort that tape out.'

Lisa flicked through her contacts and pressed the number. 'Detective Inspector Moloney's phone. Please leave a message.'

'Hi, this is Lisa Grogan. I discovered that Ruth had several nanny cams in the house. None of them show anything suspicious, but in one I can clearly hear a man threaten her. I'm anxious that as few people as possible see the recording. Can you—'

Lisa heard a loud thump coming from the kitchen.

'Mum? Are you okay?'

When there was no reply she said, 'Ring me back,' and disconnected the call. She hurried into the kitchen. Her mother was passed out on the kitchen floor.

For the second time in five months, Lisa dialled 999.

'How is she, Doctor? Is she going to be okay?'

'Your mother had a mild cardiac incident.'

'Oh God!'

'Don't worry. She's not in any immediate danger. We'll keep her in intensive care tonight, but I expect she'll be well enough to transfer to the wards tomorrow. You should get some rest, Lisa. Your mother's heavily medicated. She won't wake tonight.'

Lisa was leaving the Mater Hospital when her phone rang.

'Uncle Eamonn, it's alright, she's going to be fine.... No, there's no point coming in tonight. She won't know you're here. I'm going home myself to grab a few hours' sleep....No, no, I'm fine, really....Yes, it's a wonder she hasn't had any problems before now with all that she's had to put up with. It just goes to show how important it is that we find Shane's killer urgently. Mum can't take much more of this stress....Okay, I'll see you in the hospital tomorrow morning.'

Lisa drove home. She was almost outside her house when her phone rang. The hospital? In her panic, she nearly drove into the back of the neighbour's car and had to slam on the brakes. The car screeched to a halt. She grabbed her phone.

'Hello?...Oh, thank God, I thought you were—never mind....Yes....I only found out about it a half hour ago....

No, nobody else knows.…It's important that as few people as possible view it.…You'll understand when you see it.… I suppose that would be best. Where are you? Let me key it into my satnav.…Right, got it. I'll meet you in about forty-five minutes.'

Lisa's satnav brought her to a row of terraced, two-up two-down houses built around the 1800s. The satnav announced 'you have arrived' but she had to drive the length of the street before she found an empty parking space. It wasn't at all the kind of house she had been expecting, but a lot of areas close to the city centre were becoming increasingly gentrified. A stream of cars passed her as she walked back, but there were no pedestrians. The house she wanted was the very last in the row. A 'For Sale' sign hung from the drainpipe. As Lisa approached, she saw the note on the front door. Her heart skipped a beat.

'Idiot,' she muttered to herself. 'Is this going to be your new phobia?'

The note read 'Entrance around the back.' An arrow pointed down a narrow alley.

Lisa took out her phone and texted, 'I'm at the front door.'

Her phone pinged. 'Key got lost in move. I left the back gate open for you.'

It wasn't quite dark yet and Lisa could see the alley was deserted. Seconds later, she pushed open the black wooden gate and found herself in a tiny backyard, three-quarters of which was occupied by an overflowing skip. She squeezed past and saw the gate wasn't the only thing left open for her. The back door was also slightly ajar. Again, her heart skipped a beat. *This is not déjà vu*, she told herself. *Get a grip.*

'Hello!' she called as she rapped on the door.

A moment later, she felt a searing pain in the back of her head, followed by a loud thump. She never knew it was her head cracking against the pavement.

TWENTY-EIGHT

'HOW'S LISA'S MOTHER?' Orla asked.

'Not well enough to go to the funeral. Lisa's uncle Eamonn was there. He seems to think all the family's problems are my fault.'

'What did he say?'

'He said, "Lisa would be alive today if you had stayed out of the investigation." I figured I'd better leave as I obviously wasn't welcome. He followed me out to the car park, grabbed my arm and hissed, "My auditors have spent the last three weeks going through my books with a fine-tooth comb. So far, they've found nothing untoward. If they don't find any evidence to support the allegations you made against my son, I'm going to recommend he sues you for slander."'

'Slander? Oh, Keith fiddling his expenses? I wouldn't worry about that. But how could Eamonn blame you for Lisa's death? I thought she was mugged.'

'That's what the police say.'

'You don't believe it?'

'I don't know. It makes sense in a way. The area around the Mater is pretty rough. I've seen drug addicts hanging around there in the middle of the day.'

'And you want to believe the police are right, don't you?'

'Maybe. If Lisa wasn't mugged, then her death must be linked to the investigation. I led the investigation. What if I got her killed?'

'There's no reason to believe the investigation had anything to do with Lisa's death. Although…'

'Although what?'

'If she was murdered because of the investigation. Does that mean you're the next target?'

∽

'Great, Orla! Thanks. I hadn't thought of that.'

'Sorry, but it's worth bearing in mind, even if it's not very likely. What are the police saying? Do they have any idea who attacked Lisa?'

'No. Her body was found in an alley near the hospital, but the CCTV cameras around there didn't pick her up. Her phone, wallet and car keys were missing. They found her car burned out a few miles away. It turned out some kids had taken it for a joyride. They claim the keys were in the ignition.'

'Could they have been the ones who attacked her?'

'The police say it's unlikely. Somebody hit her over the head, but it was the blow from the ground that killed her.

The kids were pretty young and the guards know them. They don't think they would attack anybody.'

'Lisa's uncle doesn't agree?'

'Lisa told him she was going home to grab a few hours' sleep, and a neighbour saw her car outside her house later. Eamonn doesn't believe she went back to the hospital. Conor says Eamonn's been phoning him constantly, complaining the police are ignoring the murder of yet another member of his family.'

'Lisa might have grabbed some things for her mother and decided to spend the night in the hospital.'

'It's possible. I feel so sorry for that family. They have absolutely no luck. Conor checked with the Mater this morning. He says Lisa's mother is out of intensive care again but she's not doing well.'

'That poor woman. What else can go wrong for her?'

'I know. It's terrifying how a person's life can turn from normal to a nightmare in just a few months.'

'Are you carrying on with the investigation? You won't get an interview now. Especially if Lisa's uncle has turned against you.'

'I know, but Lisa would want me to continue. It might be of some comfort to her mother, and God knows that woman deserves all the comfort she can get.'

'That's for sure. How are things with Blaine?'

'I hardly see him these days. They usually come around for dinner once a week. Conor's working all hours. Blaine's started in GAA camp and he loves it. He's made new friends and he doesn't mind Conor working late.'

'How late does Conor get home?'

'Usually around ten. He thinks it might be better if Blaine went home to his mum.'

'Silver linings and all that.'

'Yes, well, Katie is worried about Blaine too. She's coming to Dublin this week to stay with them.'

'Conor's ex is going to live in Conor's house for a week?'

'Yep.'

'This is the woman Conor told Blaine he still loves?'

'That's not exactly what he said.'

'How do you feel about her staying there?'

'I trust Conor.'

'Do you trust Katie?'

TWENTY-NINE

THREE DAYS INTO Katie's visit, Aoife phoned Conor to invite them all to her home for dinner. The upbeat Australian accent was a bit of a shock.

'Detective Maloney's phone. How can I help you?'

'Katie?'

'Yes, hi. Who is this?'

'It's Aoife.'

'Oh, Aoife, hi. Conor's in the shower. Can I get him to phone you?'

'No, that's okay. I wanted to speak to you, actually.'

'I'm so glad. I've been meaning to ask Conor for your number. I want to thank you for making Blaine feel so welcome in your home.'

Was that sarcasm?

'I'm happy to have him. I phoned to invite you all to dinner tonight or any night that suits you.'

'Oh, that's so kind. I'd love to finally meet you, but

Conor and Blaine have a full schedule for me. We're having dinner in the Shelbourne tonight. I thought it would be handy for Conor as he wouldn't have far to go when he gets out of work. You're more than welcome to join us and I can't wait to meet Amy. Blaine really seems to have taken to her.'

'Thank you, but that would be a little late for Amy. Some other time, maybe? Oh, there's somebody at the door. I have to go. Bye.'

Aoife disconnected the call. Katie was answering Conor's phone? Because he was in the shower! It would never have occurred to her to touch Conor's phone, and she doubted Conor would appreciate it if she did. And Conor didn't have time to eat with her but he had time to have dinner with Katie. In the Shelbourne of all places. She'd never eaten in the Shelbourne in her life. Aoife wondered what else was included in their 'full schedule'.

'Tell me I'm being unreasonable, Orla.'

'I would if I believed it.'

'So I should be worried about Katie? What should I do?'

'Talk to Conor. Arrange for the two of you to meet alone, even if it's only for a cup of coffee. You'll know immediately if something is off.'

'And if it is?'

'We'll sort that out if it happens. In the meantime, keep yourself busy. Have you interviewed Triona yet?'

'Not yet. I plan to fit her in next week.'

'I'd do it sooner than that if I were you.'

'Why?'

'Martin isn't the only person who benefitted from Ruth's death. Triona did too.'

THIRTY

AOIFE COULDN'T PHONE Conor yet. No doubt he was still in the shower. Anyway, his evening was obviously booked. She decided to distract herself by visiting Triona.

As she drove into Leinster Square, Aoife spotted a middle-aged man in a suit and tie walking down the street. He was carrying a Bible. Aoife parked her car and watched. Triona answered the door to him, but they didn't speak long. The man moved on to her neighbour's. Aoife rang the doorbell. Triona answered it within seconds.

'Hi, could I speak to Martin, please?'

'Martin isn't here at the moment. Can I help?'

'Triona, isn't it? Hi, I'm Aoife. I called to Martin's office yesterday but he had a lunch appointment with you, so he couldn't fit me in.'

Triona looked surprised but pleased.

'I was in the area, so I thought I'd take a chance Martin was at home.'

'I'm afraid he's in the office. You're one of his clients?'

'No, although Martin has such beautiful properties on his books that I am tempted. I'm a member of Ruth's book club.'

Triona frowned.

'We were all so shocked to hear of her death.'

'Thank you. It was a real tragedy. If you'll excuse me, I have to get back to work.'

'I wondered if you had a moment to speak to me. I'm a freelance journalist and as I also knew Ruth, I plan to—'

Triona took a step backwards. 'I'm not giving interviews to reporters. If Martin wants to speak to you, that's his decision, but I have nothing to contribute to any news article.'

'Really? That man who was leaving your house as I arrived, he wasn't the main reporter for *The Sun*?'

'No, of course not, I'd never talk to anybody from that rag.'

'He didn't ask you any questions about Ruth or try to get you to invite him inside?'

'He didn't mention Ruth. He did want to come in but I said I wasn't interested. As far as I could make out, he's started his own religion and he's looking for disciples.'

Aoife laughed. 'Well, that's certainly a unique opening for a reporter. I must try it myself someday.'

'What? You mean it was a lie? He was just trying to get into the house so he could ask quest—'

Triona broke off as she spotted him across the street. 'Oh my God! He's questioning the neighbours.'

'Does he have a photographer stashed away somewhere, I wonder?'

Triona jumped back into the house and went to shut the door.

'Triona, don't throw away your chance to tell your side of the story. *The Sun* have never said a good thing about anyone. Can you imagine what they would make of a man having an affair with his murdered wife's sister? This is your opportunity to make sure everyone knows the truth.'

Triona hesitated.

Aoife handed her a business card. 'Google me. I'm not the tabloid press, and I write the truth.'

Triona took the card and closed the door in Aoife's face. Aoife sat on the doorstep and waited. Fifteen minutes later, the door opened. Triona peeked out to make sure nobody was watching the house. Opening the door wider, she said, 'Come inside. Hurry!'

Triona led the way into a room off the main corridor. Somebody, presumably Ruth, had made a huge effort to restore the room to its former grandeur. The original ceiling plasterwork and the high sash windows were beautiful. The dull, colourless portraits of somebody's long-dead ancestors made Aoife long for the bare walls she had seen on her last visit. Why would anybody want to look at those dour expressions every day? Didn't those people know how to smile? Although, in fairness, the men looked like they were being strangled by heavily starched collars that reached almost to their chins and God knows how the women moved in such restrictive outfits. Maybe it was no wonder they were in bad form. Why had Ruth chosen those paintings? Aoife was prepared to bet they had no connection whatsoever to either Ruth or Martin's family.

A giant, modern workstation in the corner looked completely out of place, as did the two large computer screens and printer and the five lever-arch files stacked against the wall.

'I work from home,' Triona said when she saw Aoife looking at them. She pointed at the sofa and took a seat opposite. 'I am not the femme fatale *The Sun* will make out. I've loved Martin since I was fifteen and he's the only man I've ever loved.'

'Fifteen! How did he end up marrying Ruth?'

'I went to college in Trinity, he went to Cork. Of course, we promised to meet up every weekend, but within a few weeks we had new lives and new friends.'

'So Martin started going out with Ruth?'

'Not for a while. There wasn't much work in Ireland at the time, so we both emigrated. We were living on opposite sides of London for a few years. The next time I saw him was at Ruth's wedding. I knew immediately that I'd made a mistake, and he's told me that he knew it too. Their marriage never stood a chance.'

'Your affair started then?'

Triona put a hand to her throat. 'You think I'd—no! I didn't want to be responsible for ruining my sister's marriage. I went back to work in London. I didn't even see

Martin again until my nephew's christening. Even when I returned to Ireland full-time, I saw them at most two or three times a year until three years ago. I'm a management consultant, and Ruth asked for my help when she decided to expand her business. That's when it happened.'

'The affair.'

'Yes. Ruth told me her marriage was a sham and that Martin had been having affairs for years. She was miserable, Martin was miserable, I was miserable. Their family was already destroyed. I figured I couldn't make things much worse. When Martin made it clear he still had feelings for me, I didn't put up much of a fight.'

'Did you consider telling Ruth?'

'No. I knew she'd never forgive me and it would cause ructions in the family. My sister hasn't spoken to me in two years and my parents barely tolerate me. That was the risk I took when we got together, but I'd hoped nobody would ever find out. I'm sorry my family are upset, but I don't regret my choice. What if Martin had been murdered as well? I'd have wasted all those years.'

'It didn't bother you that he'd cheated on Ruth?'

'I understood. He wanted something he couldn't have, so he kept looking for it in the wrong places. It wasn't easy for him living with a woman he hated.'

'Hated?'

Triona put her hand to her throat again. 'I shouldn't have said that. Martin would never have hurt Ruth. I wouldn't be with him if I thought that was even a possibility.'

'So what did you mean?'

'Martin and Ruth married for all the wrong reasons. He chose Ruth because she reminded him of me. Ruth chose him because she thought he was the type of man who would take care of her.'

'That's not Martin?'

Triona shook her head. 'Martin needs a woman to make a fuss of him. It's old-fashioned, I know, but he is who he is. If you love somebody, you have to love them faults and all.'

'Ruth couldn't do that?'

'As I said, she didn't know who she was marrying. Martin is a man of great ideas. Ruth bought into them and thought he was going places. When one after another of his businesses failed, she realised he had no idea how to carry out any of his great plans. In desperation she set up a business of her own. The more successful it became, the more she despised Martin.'

'Did Martin despise her?'

'I wouldn't say he despised her, but you can't love someone who doesn't respect you.'

'So why didn't Martin leave her?'

'He loves his kids.'

'Did he also love Ruth's money?'

Triona stood. 'I think you'd better leave now.'

THIRTY-ONE

THE FOLLOWING DAY Aoife phoned Conor and suggested they meet for coffee. 'How about someplace near your office?'

'I can't today, Aoife. It's mayhem here. I don't have a minute.'

'Tomorrow, then?'

'I wish I could but Katie's made an appointment for us to go to a photographer. She says we need some family photos. That will take at least an hour. Everyone here is working day and night. It looks really bad if I'm popping out all the time.'

'Friday, then?'

'Would you mind waiting until Sunday? I've had to take the afternoon off to drive Katie to the airport. We could drop by for dinner around six.'

'Okay, see you then.'

VAL COLLINS

෩

'Family photos!'

'Blaine is their son, Orla. That makes them a family.'

'Are you, Jason and Amy a family?'

'No.'

'Would you put off meeting Conor so you could go to a photographer to have photos taken of the three of you together?'

'I would if that was what Amy wanted.'

'You're too understanding, Aoife. Remember, that was one of your problems with Jason. You believed everything he told you.'

'Conor is not Jason.'

'I hope you're right.'

෩

It was Jason's weekend with Amy. He had phoned on Friday to say he had to work late and would collect her on Saturday morning. On Saturday he claimed his car had broken down. He would definitely collect Amy on Sunday, he promised. Amy had been upset all weekend. On Sunday she sat staring out the window, hugging Super Girl and stroking her hair. Aoife wanted to strangle Jason. She'd phoned him three times that day and each time his phone had gone to voicemail.

'Let's go for a walk, Amy.'

'No. I'm waiting for Daddy.'

Aoife was tempted to say 'Daddy can wait for you for

a change.' 'Daddy's been delayed. If his car is fixed, he'll collect you this evening. If he doesn't, you can have dinner with Conor and Blaine.'

'Blainey is coming?'

'He is. But we have time for a quick walk before he gets here.'

'We can't walk. It's raining.'

'That's why we have waterproofs, and if you put on your wellingtons, you can jump in the puddles. But only if you hurry.'

⁊

Their normal walk took twenty-five minutes. Today it took almost double that because Amy had to spend a minimum of five minutes in every single puddle.

'We have to hurry, Amy. If I don't have time to make dinner, Conor and Blaine will have to eat you.'

Amy giggled.

Aoife watched her as she climbed the fence, hands out ready to catch her if she fell.

Just as Amy's foot slipped, Aoife felt herself falling. The last thing she heard was Amy's piercing scream.

THIRTY-TWO

A STUNNED AOIFE shook her head to clear the haze. The movement caused a searing pain to shoot through her temple. When she blinked, she could make out the shadow of a man standing over her.

'You bitch! I'll teach you to call me a thief!'

'Huh?'

The man's voice was fading, growing louder and fading again. Aoife's eyes fluttered.

'Mummy!'

Aoife tried to stand, but her legs wouldn't support her body. She put her weight on her hands and rolled to one side. A voice screamed in her ear: 'How dare you ruin my life!'

A fist slammed into her head again. Aoife collapsed back on the ground. She twisted her head to look for Amy. The little girl had fallen the last two steps and landed in a heap on the ground. She picked herself up and ran towards the man, shouting, 'You leave my mummy alone!'

As Aoife tried to stand, she saw Amy pull at the man's shirt. The man reached back with one hand and pushed Amy away. He aimed his other hand at Aoife's face, but she managed to duck. The blow caught her shoulder. Aoife stumbled.

'Stop it!' Amy wailed.

As the man raised his fist again, Amy raced over, grabbed his left hand and bit it.

'Ow! Bloody brat!'

He turned around and, putting both hands on the child's shoulders, knocked her to the ground.

Aoife took an unsteady step and flung her entire body weight on the man's back.

'Leave her alone!'

The man's fist connected with Aoife's nose and she went down a third time. Her face felt like it was on fire. As the haze cleared, she saw Amy get slowly to her feet, ball her tiny hands into fists and run at the man again.

'No, Amy!' Aoife shouted. 'Conor! Get Conor!'

Amy hesitated, then raced towards home, screaming, 'Moaney! Moaney!'

Aoife prayed Conor was home by now, but at least Amy was safe. She twisted her head to one side as the man aimed another blow at her head. This time she saw his face. It was Keith.

⁂

It took a few seconds for Aoife to get to her feet again. A punch in the face sent her crashing back to the ground. Her teeth wobbled. It was only a matter of time before Keith did her serious damage. Aoife remembered an article she had read about self-defence. It said if you can't escape an attacker, roll into the tightest ball possible and protect your head at all costs. Aoife pulled her head into her knees and used her arms to protect it. Keith roared and aimed several kicks at her back. Pain shot through her, but her head was beginning to clear. She heard two pairs of feet running towards her. Conor, thank God!

But the voice she heard wasn't Conor's.

'Get your hands off my wife, you bastard!'

Jason.

Keith turned and Aoife took the opportunity to crawl out of his reach. She was on all fours, attempting to raise herself into a standing position, when she felt the boot in her back again. Aoife groaned.

'I'm talking to the police now,' Jason shouted.

Keith ignored him. He lifted his foot again and Aoife tensed, waiting for the kick. It never came. There was a whooshing sound, then a howl, and Keith landed on the ground inches from her. Aoife got to her knees. She turned in time to see someone standing over Keith, hurley raised in the air, ready to attack.

It was the very last person in the world she expected would ever help her.

THIRTY-THREE

BLAINE SWUNG THE hurley again. Keith twisted so he was flat on his back. He put out both arms, grabbed it and pulled Blaine towards him. Blaine was taken off balance and fell. Using the hurley as a crutch, Keith got to his feet and, wielding it in the air, advanced towards Blaine.

'Jason, help him!'

Jason put his phone back in his pocket. 'I called the police. They'll be here any minute.'

'Blaine needs help right now.'

Jason looked from Blaine to Keith and back to Aoife. 'You're right. Don't worry, I'll get help.'

Before she could reply, he was running across the field.

'Jason!'

He didn't even look back. Within a few seconds he was out of sight.

Aoife got to her feet and stumbled towards Keith.

Keith aimed the hurley at Blaine's head. My God, he was going to kill him.

Blaine ducked. Keith had put so much force behind the blow that he stumbled. Aoife saw her opportunity and flung her entire body weight against him. They both landed on the ground and the hurley flew out of Keith's hand. Aoife rolled off Keith's body, but he was faster getting to his feet. He reached out for the hurley. His fingers were closing on it when Blaine grabbed it and brought it down on Keith's arm. Keith swore. He flung himself at Blaine, landing on top of him and bringing them both crashing to the ground. The hurley went flying again, but Keith ignored it. He didn't need it anymore. The weight of his body kept Blaine pinned to the ground. Keith's left hand was out of action but his right fist was doing a pretty good job on Blaine's face. Aoife limped over to the hurley. She picked it up and brought it down on Keith's back. Keith howled and jumped up. Blaine scrambled to safety. He ran to Aoife, grabbed the hurley from her hand and stood in front of her as Keith charged at them. As the huge, bulky form bore down on them, Aoife muttered, 'Oh dear God!'

They didn't stand a chance.

Keith had both arms out, ready to grab the hurley, but Blaine surprised him with a jab in the stomach. Keith landed on the ground, flat on his back. Blaine raised the hurley again and brought it crashing down on Keith's knee. Aoife winced as she heard the crack. Keith screamed.

They stood looking down on Keith. Blaine held the hurley in both hands, ready to attack. But there was no fight left in Keith. He cradled his knee, screaming in pain. In between his screams, Aoife heard a high-pitched 'Mummy!' Amy was a dot in the distance. Aoife closed her eyes in relief when she saw Conor racing towards them.

THIRTY-FOUR

SEVERAL HOURS LATER, Aoife had taken aspirin and was lying on the couch. Every bone in her back ached, and it felt like her face had been broken. It wasn't, Conor assured her. She needed painkillers and rest and she'd be as right as rain in a few weeks. He gave her an ice pack and found a packet of frozen peas for Blaine.

Amy lay asleep on the couch beside her. She'd refused to let Aoife out of her sight since they'd got home. Aoife had made a big production of thanking her. 'You're such a brave girl. You stopped that bad man from hurting me.'

She made such a thing of it that Amy gradually stopped crying and began to think of herself as Super Girl who could defend the entire family all by herself. Maybe Aoife had gone a bit overboard, but it was better than having Amy cowering in a corner, terrified of every stranger she met.

The real hero, of course, was Blaine. Aoife had tried to thank him, but he'd muttered something, blushed red and left the room. Conor was practically bursting with pride.

He'd hugged Blaine. Aoife didn't hear what he said, but there was no mistaking the glow in his eyes every time he looked at his son.

Jason told everybody how lucky they were that he was there to help. Everybody but Amy ignored him. 'My daddy got help too,' she said. 'Just like me.'

Jason had the grace to look uncomfortable. Shortly afterwards he left.

∽

'Oh my God! Aoife. Are you okay?'

Aoife winced as she felt the pull on her shoulder. She switched the phone to speaker.

'Everything aches, Orla but I'll be fine.'

'Was Keith arrested?'

'Yes. Jason called the police, and a few minutes later the neighbours phoned them as well.'

'The neighbours saw what happened?'

'No. Carly's mum heard Amy screaming, so she ran around to see what was happening. She kept Amy with her while Blaine and Jason looked for me.'

'Where was Conor?'

'Traffic from the airport was quite light, so they arrived shortly after Amy and I left. They took out the hurleys and were working on Blaine's shots while they waited. When it got late, Conor went off to pick up a takeaway. Blaine was still practising when Jason arrived. A few minutes later, Amy came screaming that a bad man was hurting me.'

'You were so lucky Blaine was there to help.'

'I know. He's such a brave kid. That bastard could have killed him. I tell you I had nightmares all night about Keith aiming the hurley at Blaine's head. It's a miracle he's not dead.'

'Chip off the old block?'

'Definitely.'

'Are you friends now? Is Blaine talking to you?'

'He's not talking much at all. Conor can't figure out what's wrong with him.'

∞

Aoife called work and said she wasn't feeling well. She didn't know how they would react to her swollen and bruised face, but she wasn't in the mood to cope with their questions. She spent the best part of two days lying on the couch watching Netflix while Amy sat on the floor beside her, eyes glued to the iPad.

On the third day, Aoife decided it was time they got back to normal. Amy sulked because she wasn't allowed the iPad, but she soon settled down and Aoife tackled her growing pile of ironing. Twenty minutes later, she realised the house was too quiet and went in search of Amy. She found her crouched behind the sofa, jabbing at the iPad.

'Amy! Where did you get that?'

A wide-eyed Amy replied, 'I don't know.'

'You don't know? Give it to me, please.'

She went to switch it off and realised the iPad didn't belong to her.

'Is this Blaine's?'

Amy shrugged.

'You are not allowed touch the iPad unless I give it to you, and you are not ever allowed to touch Blaine's things. Are you listening to me?'

Tears sprang into Amy's eyes and she ran out of the room.

Aoife looked at the photo Amy had been examining: Katie, Conor and Blaine. They seemed happy. Blissfully happy actually, like the family photos you see in adverts. Conor's arm was around Katie's waist and she smiled up at him. Good God! Aoife flicked through photo after photo of her partner and his perfect family. She gritted her teeth. Katie was slim and beautiful with that sun-kissed look no Irish person could ever achieve. Conor appeared to be the proud family man and Blaine was happy and relaxed. Several of the photos were taken in Stephen's Green. In one, Katie was waving a hurley in the air while her son and his father cheered. Aoife snorted. As if Katie knew about hurling! Conor had told her that Katie hadn't even known what a hurley was until Blaine asked for one as a birthday present. When their local sports shop didn't sell any, she had bought him a hockey stick, thinking it would be a suitable alternative. Aoife flicked to the next photo and froze.

'What the hell!'

This was a much older photo. Blaine was about thirteen. He and Conor were standing on a beach. Conor had his arm around Blaine and they both smiled into the camera. Beside them, standing so close to Conor that they almost touched and wearing a bikini that left very little to the imagination, was Lisa.

THIRTY-FIVE

'LISA! WHAT WAS Lisa doing on a beach with Conor and Blaine?'

'I have no idea. Lisa mentioned that she had been living with a guy, but it never even occurred to me that it was Conor. She always referred to him as Detective Moloney. Do you think that means something? I always call him Conor. Wouldn't it have been natural for her to start calling him Conor too? Now that I think about it—'

'What?'

'Maybe I'm being stupid, Orla, but I remember the very first time I saw Lisa in the restaurant, my immediate impression was that they had a personal relationship.'

'Why did you think that?'

'It was the way she spoke to him. All I caught was "not answering my calls" and "what do I have to do to get". I assumed she said "what do I have to do to get your attention" or "what do I have to do to get you to return my calls".'

'She could have said either of those things, but it wouldn't necessarily mean they were a couple.'

'I know. Later, after Lisa spoke to me, I asked Conor about the case. He didn't want to talk about it. Then he got a text message on his phone. I remember him frowning at it. Then he said okay, he'd fill me in on the background. What if that text was a message from Lisa? What if she said she would tell me they had been a couple if Conor didn't let me help her?'

'But why wouldn't Conor want you to know Lisa was his ex? You said Blaine was about thirteen in the photo. You hadn't even met Conor then.'

'The photo was taken about two years ago, but Lisa broke up with her ex a few months before Shane and his family were murdered. Conor was pressurising me to get engaged then. Surely he wasn't double-timing me?'

'You're going to have to talk to Blaine. If Lisa and Conor were an item, Blaine must know all about it.'

Aoife left Amy with her grandmother and drove to Dublin. She parked outside Conor's house until Blaine returned from GAA camp.

'Hi, Blaine,' she called as he was opening the front door.

Blaine turned. Aoife felt a stab of pity when she saw the purple and black bruises that covered his face. His expression was wary and something else. Did she see fear? Why would Blaine be afraid of her?

'You left this in my house the night we were attacked.'

Blaine took the iPad. 'Thanks.'

'Can I come in?'

'Dad's at work.'

'I know. I'd like to speak to you.'

'What! Why?'

'There's no need to look so worried. I just wanted to ask you about a photo.'

'A photo!'

'It will only take a minute.'

Blaine opened the door and went straight upstairs. She heard the bathroom door shut. A few minutes later the loo flushed, she heard running water and he was downstairs again.

'Blaine, Amy found your iPad. When I took it from her, she was looking at your photos. There was one of you and your dad on the beach with a woman.'

Blaine shrugged.

'Who is the woman, Blaine?'

'I don't know. I don't know what photo you're talking about.'

'Can I show it to you?'

Blaine handed her the iPad. Aoife flicked through the photos.

The photo of Lisa was no longer there.

৵

'Blaine, why did you delete the photo?'

'I don't know what you're talking about. I didn't delete anything.'

'When I handed you the iPad, there was a photo of you, your dad and a woman on the beach. It isn't there now. Where did it go?'

Blaine shrugged.

'Blaine, did you know Lisa?'

'Who's Lisa?'

Aoife took out her phone and brought up a newspaper article about the bad luck that followed the Grogan family. She showed the photo to Blaine.

'Do you know her?'

Blaine nodded.

'How do you know her?'

'She came to your house a while back and asked me where you worked.'

'Had you ever seen her before then?'

Blaine shook his head.

'So why did you have a photo of her on the beach with you and your dad?'

'I didn't. Why would I want a photo of that woman? I have to go out now. My friends are waiting for me.'

If Orla was free, she and Aoife met up whenever Aoife was in Dublin. Aoife was reluctant to meet her today. She was uncomfortable displaying her bruised face to strangers, but she needed to discuss her worries. Fallon & Byrne was out of the question. Too many people there knew them. Until her face was back to normal, Aoife wanted anonymity. They arranged to meet in the food hall in the Stephen's Green Shopping Centre. Aoife went to the noodle stand and got her favourite meal of rice noodles with prawns and peanuts, topped with sesame seeds. She took the tray upstairs and chose a window seat. She was looking down at the Luas, wondering about the lives of its passengers, when Orla joined her.

Once Orla had recovered from the shock of seeing her friend's battered face, Aoife told her about her encounter with Blaine.

'He denied ever seeing it?'

'Yep.'

'What are you going to do now?'

'I don't know. Ask Conor, I imagine.'

'Are you sure that's a good idea?'

'Why not?'

'Think about it. Conor must have known Lisa, yet he kept that a secret from you. Why?'

'That's what I intend to find out.'

'And what if you find out that Conor has been lying to you all this time? He double-timed you with Lisa. He dumped you the minute Katie arrived in town and now his ex-girlfriend is dead.'

'We don't know if any of that is true, Orla.'

'We know Blaine wants to split up you and Conor. Agreed?'

Aoife nodded.

'The photo of Conor and Lisa would be the perfect weapon. All he has to do is tell you Conor and Lisa were an item, but he doesn't. Why not?'

'I don't know.'

'He doesn't say anything because he's afraid. You said yourself that you saw fear in his eyes. Blaine's scared Conor was involved in Lisa's death.'

'No, he isn't. Even if Conor was two-timing me, why would he want Lisa dead?'

'I have no idea, but I never met Lisa and I don't know Conor very well.'

'I know Conor extremely well and I'm telling you he didn't have anything to do with Lisa's death.'

'You've only known him a little over a year, Aoife. Blaine's known him a hell of a lot longer and he's worried enough to delete that photo.'

'Maybe Blaine deleted the photo to annoy me. He hid my stuff, now he's hiding his own stuff from me.'

'No. Blaine was annoying you in the hope that you and Conor would argue. The photo is much more likely to cause an argument, yet he hides it.'

'What exactly are you trying to say, Orla?'

'I'm saying it's possible you don't know Conor as well as you think you do. It's even possible he's violent.'

'That's nonsense. How could you say such a thing? I thought you liked Conor.'

'I did like him. But I've been wrong about men before. So have you.'

'Conor would never hurt anybody.'

'How sure are you of that?'

'One hundred percent.'

'Like you were one hundred percent certain that Jason was the perfect husband?'

THIRTY-SIX

'DON'T COMPARE CONOR to Jason. They're almost a different species, Orla.'

'Are you sure? You have a habit of only seeing the good in people you love. I tried to warn you about Jason when we were in college, remember? You didn't want to know then either.'

'I don't remember you saying anything about Jason.'

'That's because you weren't listening. I told you he was cutting you off from all your friends and you'd be better off without him. You couldn't see what was in front of your face then either.'

'That was completely different. I was a kid who'd just lost both her parents. I needed something to cling to, and Jason took advantage of that. I'm an adult now.'

'Lots of adults fall in love with the wrong men.'

'Conor isn't the wrong man, Orla. I'm certain of it.'

※

But was she certain? Feeling like a complete traitor, Aoife decided to visit Lisa's uncle. The receptionist was gone, but several employees were still milling around. Aoife ignored their shocked expressions and went straight to Eamonn's office. She knocked at the door.

'Come in.'

Eamonn paled at the sight of Aoife's swollen and bruised face. 'I'm sorry.' He got up and pulled out a chair for her. 'I can't believe Keith did that. I don't know what came over him. Did you come here because I paid his bail?'

'He's out on bail?'

'I had to pay it, Aoife. He's my son. But I swear you have nothing to worry about. I told Keith he will have to find another job if he goes within ten miles of you.'

'I need your help, Eamonn.'

'Anything.'

'Do you have photos of Lisa's ex?'

'No.'

'Do you know what he looked like?'

'She brought him to a family wedding, but I didn't pay much attention.'

Aoife took out her phone and held up a photo of Conor. As Lisa's murder had been deemed a mugging, the investigation was being handled by the local police station. Aoife knew Eamonn had spoken to Conor, but she was pretty sure they'd never met. In any case, Conor looked quite different in jeans and a T-shirt and without his hair gelled back.

'Is this him?'

Eamonn examined the photo.

'I don't know. He's the right age and about the right height and the hair is the same colour, but I don't remember his features. Like I said, there were a lot of people at the wedding. I barely glanced at him.'

'Can you give me the number of any of Lisa's friends?'

'I don't have a clue who her friends were. Her mother would know, of course, but I can't upset her now. She's barely surviving as it is.'

'No, of course not. How about her work colleagues? Where did Lisa work?'

'I've definitely heard her mention the name of the company, but I can't think of it off the top of my head. I know they went into liquidation a few months ago.'

'And I don't suppose you know the name of any of her work colleagues.'

'I'm sorry, Aoife. Keith and Lisa never got on. She stayed away from my family as much as possible. We met at weddings and funerals. That was about it.'

Before going to bed, Aoife searched the web for a Facebook or Instagram profile belonging to Lisa. She found several Lisa Grogans. A surprising number of them lived in New Zealand. None were the Lisa she wanted. As many of Aoife's friends had profiles under their Irish names, Aoife did another search. She found Lisa O Grugain and Lisa Ni Ghrugain. They were all strangers.

Aoife slept badly. She was due back at work the following day and her face was still a mess. What was she going to tell people when they asked what had happened to her? Nobody at her office job knew she was a freelance reporter, and she preferred to keep her two lives separate. But if she didn't tell them, how could she explain her appearance? Aoife could have saved herself the worry. Her colleagues noticed her bruised and swollen face, their eyes widened and they immediately looked away. Nobody asked what happened to her. The realisation that they assumed her partner was beating her up came as a shock. It was an even greater shock that not one person asked if she was alright.

After work, Aoife collected Amy and dropped her at her grandmother's. Conor had agreed to meet her when his shift ended and she was going to ask him straight out about the photo. They were having dinner at 8 p.m., so she had a few hours to spare. She washed her hair and tried on a few outfits. Why was she bothering? It's unlikely there was a correct way to dress to ask your partner if he had double-timed you.

One of the advantages of long, straight hair was there was never any need to blow-dry it. Aoife threw on a pair of jeans and a top and headed for her office. Her hand was out to pull back the latch when she saw it wasn't fully drawn across. That was weird. She always pushed it fully across and then checked that it was shut. It was a habit she had developed after Amy, aged two, had spilled juice all over her keyboard. Aoife had been working in the office the previous evening and left her charger there. She had gone in that morning and collected it. Maybe she hadn't bolted it properly in the rush. Aoife opened the door and peeked inside. At first glance, everything seemed untouched, but as she got closer, she noticed her solar-powered keyboard was switched on. It had died on her once, and she'd spent the following day trying to type whilst aiming the keyboard at the sun. Ever since, she had been meticulous about switching it off. Blaine had definitely been here. Who else would break into her house and take nothing? Aoife dialled Conor's mobile.

'Hi.'

'Hi, things are a bit hectic here, but I promise I'll be at the restaurant at eight on the dot.'

'Great. Conor, I hate to say this, especially after everything he did for me, but I think Blaine was in my house today.'

'What?'

'The latch to the door in my office wasn't fully drawn across and my keyboard was switched on. I never leave my keyboard on.'

'Aoife, I don't believe you! Blaine risked his life to save you and you accuse him of breaking into your house. How would he even get to Kildare?'

'He could have taken the train.'

'This is ridiculous, Aoife, and it's got to stop. You forgot

VAL COLLINS

to turn off your keyboard and you immediately blame my son. My son who could have been seriously injured trying to save you. How you could say—I don't know, Aoife. I really don't know what's wrong with you.'

'Conor, please listen to me. I don't want to accuse Blaine, but there's nobody else who could have done this.'

'You did it, Aoife. You're absent-minded. That's it. Stop blaming other people for your mistakes.'

'I know you don't want to believe it, Conor, but Blaine was in my house today. I'm certain of it.'

'I put Blaine on a flight to England last night. He was in his mother's house when I phoned this morning. Let's forget about dinner, Aoife. I've lost my appetite. Goodbye.'

Goodbye? As in goodbye forever?

'Conor?'

The line was dead.

Aoife phoned Orla, but she didn't pick up. If Blaine hadn't been in her house, then who had? She'd changed the locks after Jason had left. Could he have got a hold of her new key? If he'd been in the area, he would have called to his mother. Aoife rang Maura.

'Hi, Maura, Conor's cancelled on me, so I'll come by and pick up Amy shortly.'

'Oh, don't do that, Aoife. I promised Amy we'd bake a cake and she's very excited at the idea of bringing you home something nice. Why not leave her here for a few hours? I'm sure you could do with some time to yourself.'

'Okay, if you're certain you don't mind. Maybe Jason could join you for a while. Amy was upset she missed his last visit.'

'I know. The poor little kid. I'm so sorry. That was entirely my fault. I was getting over a bug. I thought I'd be better by Saturday, but it was Sunday afternoon before I could drag myself out of bed. To be honest, I thought it would be a good opportunity for Jason to discover he could manage Amy on his own. He's still a little nervous.'

'Nervous?'

'You know what men are like. They have no idea what to do when a little girl cries. The first weekend Amy visited, she cried for you the entire time. Jason rang me in a state. He insists I'm there for every visit now.'

'I had no idea. I mean, I knew you saw Amy every weekend and I knew you were in Jason's house, but I didn't realise you spent the entire weekend with them.'

'Oh yes. I'm sure Jason will get over his panic in time, but for the moment I couldn't be happier. I can never have too much of my favourite granddaughter.'

'Right. Do you think Jason will call by tonight?'

'No, Aoife, I'm afraid he can't. He's at a conference in Kerry. It's his first big presentation. His company are running something or other on Facebook. I can't remember what it's called, but Jason set it up for me. If you click on it, you can hear all the speeches. I listened to Jason's this morning, and later I watched when he was given his award. Isn't technology amazing?'

'Amazing.'

Aoife put her head in her hands. Okay, so Jason hadn't been in her house and neither had Blaine. What kind of a burglar breaks into a house, switches on a keyboard and leaves? It had to be somebody who wanted to get into her computer. What was on her computer that would interest anybody? She had the notes of her interviews, but who would care about those? Other than the murderer, of course. Had the murderer been in her house? Oh my God! Had he come to kill her?

THIRTY-SEVEN

AOIFE RANG ORLA again. Still no answer. Where the hell was she? Aoife told herself to calm down. She had to think about this rationally. She didn't believe Triona would murder anybody, so the murderer was either Martin or Keith. Martin had said he wanted to smash Shane's head in, and Triona confirmed he didn't like Ruth. But why would he kill Shane's family? Keith, on the other hand, had viciously attacked her. Given a chance, he might have killed both her and Blaine. Was it so much of a stretch to believe he'd killed Shane's family? Blaine was older than Shane's kids, but he was still a kid. Keith hadn't thought twice about attacking him. But what could either Keith or Martin want from her computer?

The floor creaked and Aoife jumped. She picked up her phone, keyed in 999 and waited, thumb hovering over the button. Nothing. The tension in her body eased a little once she realised it was just the normal creaking of an old house. When she was sure there was no intruder, Aoife jumped up. She flew from room to room, throwing clothes, toys and toiletries into a bag. Then she grabbed her laptop and ran to her car. The next time the murderer came looking for her, all he would find was an empty house.

THIRTY-EIGHT

AOIFE WAS CHECKING into the hotel when Orla phoned.

'Aoife, I have to tell you about this new guy in the office. We went out last night and I really think I'm in love. Honestly, he looks nothing like a lawyer. Think Liam Hemsworth and—Aoife, are you listening to me?'

'Hmm? Oh, yes, sorry, Liam Hemsworth. What about him?'

'What's wrong?'

'Nothing.'

'I know something is wrong, Aoife, I can hear it in your voice.'

'I had to move out of the house. Amy and I are checking into a hotel.'

'Why?'

'The murderer was in my house. I think he came there to kill me.'

❧

'I want to go home!'

'We're on holidays, Amy. Nobody spends their holidays at home. This is a really nice hotel. You'll love it.'

'I won't. I want to go home.'

'You wouldn't like to go to the teddy bear tea party?'

❧

Amy kept a small yellow teddy bear clamped under her arm as she swapped teddy-bear-shaped sandwiches with her new best friend.

As Aoife watched, a vision of herself and Amy kept popping into her head. They were lying on the kitchen floor, arms and legs stretched wide. The white tiles were red with their blood, and a knife lay on the floor between them.

Should she go to the police? And tell them what? A not-fully-engaged latch and a switched-on keyboard were not evidence. They'd take her statement and file it somewhere with reports they received from people with mental health issues. What hope did she have of convincing a stranger? She hadn't even been able to convince Conor there had been a break-in.

Her phone beeped and she jumped several inches into the air. One of the other mums glanced at her, then moved to the other side of the room. Great, now she was giving off crazy-lady vibes.

The text was from Orla.

'All okay?'

'Fine. With Amy.'

'Was thinking about what you said. Have password on home computer?'

'No need.'

'Maybe murderer not interested in computer at all. It was there. Easy to get at. Anybody would be curious.'

'Going to search computer anyway. Will read every single document. See if anything missed.'

'That will take a while.'

'Don't have a while. Have to find murderer before he comes after us again. Resigned work this morning. Now either with Amy or working on this.'

'Can you afford to resign?'

'No. Better broke than dead.'

✧

Orla's text had made Aoife restless. She wanted to start checking her computer that second. Her fight or flight reflex was still engaged and standing around doing nothing was agony. But there was something she could do now, Aoife realised. She could check emails on her phone. Aoife began the long process of opening and reading every email. She took a short break to pose with Amy, the yellow teddy bear and a plate of teacup-shaped biscuits. Later, as Aoife examined the photo, she thought what a shame it was that Lisa would never have children. That was when it struck her. Lisa had sent her an email the day she'd died. Aoife had seen the email arrive, titled 'List of Ruth's phone calls'. Figuring Lisa would have phoned her if there was anything worth mentioning, Aoife had ignored it and later forgot it existed.

She flicked through her emails, searching for it. The email was gone.

❦

Somebody didn't want her to know who Ruth had called the day she'd died. Why?

Aoife went into the corridor to make her call, standing at the window, where she could keep an eye on Amy, who was enjoying her first game of musical chairs.

'Hi, Eamonn….I'm fine, but I need an email Lisa sent me. It disappeared from my laptop. Do you have access to her computer?…She didn't have one?…Well, yes, I suppose a lot of people rely entirely on their phones these days. Her phone was stolen, wasn't it?…Did she have an automatic back-up system on it? Could you check?…Yeah, I know. There are new things every day, aren't there? Do you have somebody who handles your IT?…An entire department, brilliant. Can you get them to work on it? I'll text you my email address. If they could resend Lisa's last email to me, that would be great. Oh, could they send me her call log too? Thanks, Eamonn.'

If Lisa relied entirely on her phone, it was almost certain that she had a backup system. It should be easy enough for an IT department to get into it, shouldn't it?

Maybe it would be better to have insurance. She checked the text she had sent Lisa with Frank O'Meara's contact details and dialled the number.

'Hi, I'm a colleague of Lisa Grogan. You provided us with a list of calls made by Ruth Kin—'

'I have no idea what you're talking about.'

The call was disconnected.

Aoife waited twenty minutes. She fixed her phone so her number was withheld and dialled again. She guessed that a man in Frank O'Meara's line of business would have to answer calls from numbers he didn't recognise.

'If you hang up on me, I will come to Harcourt Street and have our conversation there in full view of your colleagues.'

'What?'

'All I want is a copy of the list you gave Lisa.'

Aoife heard a door bang and traffic in the background.

'I am out of that line of business. Do not phone me again.'

Aoife raised her voice to be heard over the traffic.

'I paid for that list and I want a copy. You can agree to give me one now, or I can come to your office.'

'Listen to me,' the voice hissed. 'I can't get you the list. The original has disappeared from the DI's computer. All hell has broken loose here. They've called in all kinds of experts to examine the DI's machine, but they can't recover the list.'

'Didn't they get the information in the first place from Ruth's phone provider? Why not get it again?'

'Somebody in that company opened a dodgy email and their entire system crashed. They're trying to recover it, but it could take weeks and there's a good chance that info is gone for good.'

'But I paid—'

'It doesn't matter what you paid for. If anyone found out I gave you that list, I'd lose my job at the very least. I might even end up in jail. Everybody here is under suspicion. Even the DI.'

'The DI?'

'Detective Inspector Moloney.'

THIRTY-NINE

CONOR WAS UNDER suspicion? It might explain why he hadn't been in touch yet, assuming he intended to contact her again, of course. No, she was being stupid. Conor obviously had a lot on his mind. Aoife felt bad for adding to his troubles. She felt even worse when she woke the next morning to find an email from Eamonn with a copy of the missing list. Should she forward it to Conor? Okay, she really shouldn't make decisions before breakfast. That was an incredibly stupid idea. It would make everything much worse for Conor. Everyone would think he'd given her the numbers. All she could do was go through the list herself. If she discovered anything of interest, she would have to find a way to let Conor know.

Aoife dropped Amy at Maura's and settled down to her task. Not knowing what cover story Lisa had used for phoning them, Aoife went with a version of the truth. She was a reporter doing a story on Ruth and she was checking to see if any of Ruth's friends would like to provide backstory.

The occasional person reacted with shock and horror, but even they said enough to clarify their relationship with Ruth. Most were happy to talk at length about how dangerous the world had become and how shocked they had been by the murder.

Aoife left Natasha, the nanny, until last. It was hard to know what to say. Lisa and Natasha had obviously spoken, but what name had Lisa given and what cover story had she used? Aoife decided to go with the journalist line. If that didn't work, she'd leave it a day or so and try another cover story.

The nanny had laughed. 'Sorry, I can't talk to a journalist about my ex-boss. Dublin is a very small city. I'd never work again.'

Aoife decided she would break for lunch and then go through Ruth's phone calls. She brought a sandwich back to her room, made a cup of coffee and switched on the TV while she ate. A rerun of *Friends* provided background noise without demanding too much attention. Aoife was half listening to Ross and Rachel argue about being on a break and half checking Lisa's phone log. She had spent quite some time talking to the nanny. Maybe the nanny required urgent attention. When Aoife's eyes landed on the final number, her sandwich slipped from her hand and she almost sent her coffee flying. The very last person Lisa had contacted was Conor.

FORTY

AOIFE WAS ON the verge of tears when she phoned Orla. She could hear the hesitancy in Orla's voice and realised she'd rung at a bad time. Aoife knew she should say it wasn't urgent and they would talk when Orla was free, but she couldn't bring herself to do it. She needed help right now.

Orla didn't have time for a sit-down lunch, so they bought crepes in the Lemon Crepe on Suffolk Street and took them into the grounds of Trinity College. They joined a handful of students enjoying the sun on the steps of the Dining Hall.

'That's not good, Aoife.'

Aoife caught a bit of cheese that was about to fall out of her crepe.

'I knew you were going to say that.'

'Because you know I'm right.'

'There's some simple explanation I'm not getting.

I need you to help me work it out. Take my word for it that Conor is not involved and try to come up with other possibilities.'

'What I think is'—Orla balanced the crepe on one knee and counted out with her fingers—'One, Conor was on a beach with Lisa. Two, he denied knowing her. Three, his own son is scared and deleted the photo. Four, the very last person Lisa spoke to was Conor. Five, somebody deleted the email Lisa sent you with Ruth's phone calls from your computer. Who has easier access to your computer than Conor?'

She tried to change hands and almost sent the crepe flying. 'Why don't they give you paper plates for these? This is ridiculous.' She wiped her hands with a tissue. 'Where was I? Oh, right.' She counted out on her left hand. 'Six, the day Lisa sent that email, she was murdered. Seven, the last person she spoke to was Conor. Eight, the original list has now disappeared from Conor's computer.'

'I know it doesn't look good, Orla, but—'

'You heard what that O'Meara guy said, Aoife. Conor is under suspicion from his own police department. The top police investigation unit in the country think he's up to something.'

Aoife's head was spinning. Conor would never kill anybody. She was absolutely positive about that. Orla didn't understand because she didn't really know Conor. Jenny had known Conor longer than Aoife had. If he had been going out with Lisa, it was possible Jenny would know. Even if she'd never met Lisa herself, she was obviously kept up to date about the department's gossip.

'You're in town? Great! Pop over and we'll have a chat.'

Aoife picked up a packet of M&S éclairs. She wasn't a huge fan of shop-bought cakes, even M&S cakes, but their éclairs were almost as good as the real thing. If she was hunting for information, the least she could do was bring payment of a sort.

∾

'Ooh, I love these. You're not doing much for my diet, Aoife.'

'I needed something to cheer myself up.'

'What's wrong?'

'Lots of things. Conor for one.'

'You had a fight?'

Aoife nodded.

'Do you want to tell me about it?'

'It was a misunderstanding about his son. Jenny, have you ever met any of the women Conor dated before me?'

'No, I don't think so. I heard Blaine's mother visited recently. Is that what the argument was about?'

'It didn't help. Have you met Katie?'

'No. Did it bother you that she stayed in Conor's house?'

'Not at first, but when I rang looking for Conor, she answered his phone. It really felt like they were a couple. And then they went to a photographer for some family photos.'

'I can't say I know what you're going through, Aoife. I was Derek's first serious girlfriend, but I think you may be getting upset over nothing. Every time I've seen you together, Conor only has eyes for you.'

'Katie answered his phone, Jenny. It would never even occur to me to touch Conor's phone.'

'I answer Derek's phone sometimes if he leaves it lying around. He answers mine. Katie is married, isn't she?'

'Yes.'

'Maybe she's in the habit of answering her husband's phone and she picked it up without thinking. I'm sure you have nothing to worry about.'

'I hope you're right.'

Jenny laughed. 'I'm always right. Didn't you know?' She helped herself to another éclair. 'How's the investigation going?'

'Terrible. I don't seem to be getting anywhere with it.'

'Of course you're getting somewhere, Aoife. In the beginning you thought Shane killed himself and his family. You know that's not true now.'

'Everybody knows that since Ruth was murdered.'

'Yeah, I can't believe she had a thing for Shane. I never guessed it. Although maybe I should have. She always started the WhatsApp discussions and occasionally she'd join in with one or two comments, but the one time Shane got involved, she was commenting every few minutes.'

'What were they talking about?'

'Remember, I told you about it. It was the time we were discussing *Gone with the Wind*.'

'Do you still have those messages?'

'Sure.'

Jenny scrolled through her messages until she found the correct one. The discussion had started calmly enough. The first question, posted by Ruth, was 'Did Ashley love Scarlett or Melanie?' Most people felt he loved Melanie. Shane felt differently. He believed Ashley loved Scarlett. He'd chosen to marry Melanie because she was a safer bet. When Jenny disagreed with him, he replied, 'Like must marry like or there'll be no happiness'.

As Aoife flicked through the messages, she saw the tone change. Shane was more insistent that only racists could possibly enjoy a book that claimed freedom was very hard for slaves and they had a better life under the protection of their masters. Several outraged replies later, Ruth had closed down the thread.

'The night they discussed that book, you said the arguments got very intense.'

'Oh yes. Shane's insistence that half the group were racists didn't help. He was getting quite annoyed. It was a good thing he was interrupted by a phone call. Although the call made him even angrier. When he left the room, Ruth took advantage of his absence to move the conversation to a discussion of our next read. Then, of course, Shane came back with the cake and everybody relaxed.'

'Do you know who phoned him?'

'No, but Bronagh might. She was sitting beside him when he took the call.'

❧

Bronagh's husband, Ed, was not at all what Aoife had expected. As broad as he was tall, he was the perfect build for a rugby hooker. About the only trait he shared with his wife was the complete absence of fat. Were the entire family fitness addicts?

'Hi, could I speak to Bronagh, please?'

'She's tied up at the moment. Can I help?'

'I'm Aoife. Bronagh and I spoke about Shane Grogan's death. I would really appreciate it if I could have a quick word. It won't take a minute.'

'The investigator? My wife has nothing to say to you. She was very upset by Ruth's death. If you think she's the murderer, you're barking up the wrong tree.'

'I wanted to speak to her about the book club.'

'Oh! Well, you'd better come in, then. Bronagh's out the back,' Ed said, walking ahead.

Aoife followed him into the back garden.

'Ed, this is ridiculous.' Bronagh banged the root of a large thistle against the wall and let the excess earth fall into the rose bed. 'Wouldn't you think that after all these years, somebody would have come up with a better way to remove weeds? I mean, how is it possible that we can send a man to the moon but—oh, hi, Aoife.'

'I wonder if we could have a chat.'

'What about?'

'I'd like to ask you a question about the book club.'

A broad smile lit up Bronagh's face.

'Sure.'

She removed a pair of gardening gloves, turned them inside out and stuffed them in the pocket of her cargo pants. 'I'm covered in dirt. Let's sit down out here.'

She led the way to two sun loungers in the centre of the garden. Bronagh perched on one edge and Aoife sat opposite.

'Heavens, it's hot.' Pulling at her skintight orange top, Bronagh said, 'I hope you don't think it's insensitive of me to take over running the book club, Aoife. What happened to Ruth was awful, but I'm sure she would want the book club to continue. It meant a great deal to her, and she would be appalled by the suggestions that we should disband it. I know she'd approve of my plans to make it something really special.'

'That would be great. I'm looking forward to hearing your ideas but right now I need to ask you about a book club meeting that took place a few weeks before the Grogans were murdered.'

'Oh! I'd rather concentrate on the future, but if you must.'

'Thank you. The meeting I'm interested in is the one where you discussed *Gone with the Wind*. In the middle of the discussion, Shane got a phone call. I understand he seemed quite angry, and I've been told you were sitting beside him when he took the call. Do you know who he was speaking to?'

'Somebody from work. He called him Keith.'

'You heard the conversation?'

'Not at first. I heard a man on the other end of the phone, shouting. Shane went out to the kitchen, and later I passed him on my way to the bathroom. That's when I heard him call the man Keith.'

'Did you hear anything else?'

Bronagh nodded. 'Shane said, "They were waiting for me in the car park, Keith. We have the same surname. We work for the same company."'

'That was all you heard?'

'Those are the only full sentences. Then Shane said "What?" but a car drove by, so I missed most of it. All I caught was "come to my house".'

Aoife almost ran back to her car she was so anxious to speak to Orla.

'"What if they come to my house? Or "What if they had come to my house?" It has to be one or the other, Orla. What else could it be?'

'You think it might have been an organised crime murder after all? They were coming for Keith because he owed money, but they got the wrong Grogan?'

'I don't know. It was weeks before the murder. Presumably Shane explained that they had the wrong person. Why would they make the same mistake again?'

'Maybe they had already given out the incorrect address and they forgot to change it, or the change of address was never communicated to the right person. Or maybe Keith owed money to more than one criminal.

FORTY-ONE

IT HAD NOT been a very productive day. Aoife was running out of time. Who knew when the murderer would come looking for her again? She needed to talk to somebody who knew both Natasha and Ruth. The only person she could think of was Ruth's sister, Susan.

It took Aoife a while to find Susan on Instagram. A quick glance through her photos and there wasn't much she didn't learn about Susan's life, including the fact that, like many people who worked in the area, she regularly ate her lunch in the gardens of Dublin Castle.

The following day, Aoife was in the park at twelve-thirty. It had rained earlier, so it was unlikely Susan would be sitting on the grass. A quick search of the few benches and Aoife found her.

Susan looked up from her book when Aoife joined her.

'What do you want?'

'I was sorry to hear about Ruth. I could tell you two were very close.'

'I'm not giving you an interview if that's what you're after.'

'The only thing I'm interested in is finding Shane and Ruth's murderer.'

'And how do you intend to do that?'

'With your help.'

'If I knew anything, I would have told the police.'

'How well do you know Natasha?'

Susan closed her book and turned to face Aoife. 'You get around, don't you? Who told you about that little tramp?'

'I take it you're not a fan.'

Susan shrugged. 'I told Ruth it was madness hiring that girl. Have you seen her?'

Aoife shook her head.

'She's like a blonde Barbara Palvin. I'm not saying she wasn't good with the kids. She was excellent, actually, but she was a magnet for men of all ages. It was bound to cause trouble.'

'She had men in the house?'

'Natasha didn't live in Ruth's house. But Ruth often attended functions and she didn't get home until the early hours of the morning. Once the kids were in bed, Natasha got bored. She usually found someone to entertain her.'

'What did Ruth think of that?'

'So long as the kids didn't see it, Ruth was prepared to put up with it, until she went too far.'

'Too far?'

'One day Martin came by to see the kids. He stayed around until the kids were in bed and ended up on the sofa with Natasha.'

'Ruth walked in on them?'

'No. She never did tell me how she found out. I think one of the kids must have seen them.'

'What happened?'

'Ruth fired Natasha. Natasha got her revenge by telling Ruth that Martin and Triona were living together.'

'How did she know?'

'She said she heard him on the phone asking Triona if she had paid the rent. Ruth was livid. Not only was Martin living with her sister but he had found another member of the family to support him.'

'What did Ruth do?'

'She threatened to tell Triona about Natasha. It always drove Ruth crazy that Triona believed she was Martin's one true love. She was pretty sure Martin would have to find another woman to live off once Triona learned the truth.'

'How did Martin react?'

'He said if Ruth spoke to Triona it would be the last thing she ever did.'

FORTY-TWO

AMY WAS TIRED of hotel life. She wanted her own bedroom, her toys, her friends at kindergarten, Conor and Blaine.

When Aoife was putting her to bed that night, she said, 'Is Blainey with his mummy now?'

'Yes, he is.'

'Is he in England?'

'Yes.'

'I want him to live in Ireland.'

'He has to live with his mummy.'

'I want Moaney to live in Ireland too.'

'Conor lives in Ireland, Amy. You know that.'

'Daddy says Moaney's going to live with Blainey and his mummy now.'

'When did Daddy say that?'

'Lots of times. Blainey said it too.'

'Blaine told you Conor and his mummy were going to live together?'

'No, he told Daddy. Or Daddy told Blainey. I don't remember.'

Oh God! What was Jason up to now?

Aoife knelt on the floor so she was eye level with Amy.

'Sweetie, what did Daddy say to Blaine?'

'He said—I don't remember. Lots of things. I want a story.'

'Okay, sweetie. Let's get out your book. What story do you want tonight?'

There was no point in trying to get any more information from Amy. She would have to speak to Blaine. She phoned the hotel reception, explained she couldn't leave her daughter alone and asked if somebody would go to the supermarket and buy her a cheap phone as she had left hers at home. She wanted a number Blaine wouldn't recognise. Aoife made sure Amy was fast asleep, then she called him.

'Hi.'

'Hi, Blaine.'

'Aoife?'

'Yes, it's me.'

'What do you want?'

'I want to talk to you.'

'I can't talk now. I'm busy.'

'Blaine, if you hang up, I'm going to phone your mum.'

She was bluffing, of course. She didn't even know

Katie's number, and asking Conor for it would lead to questions she wasn't yet in a position to answer.

'Why do you want to speak to Mum?'

'I don't really. I'd much rather speak to you.'

'Why?'

'I want to talk about the conversations you've been having with Jason.'

'What conversations?'

'Amy told me about them.'

'Amy was listening?'

'Kids always listen. You know that. You listen to Conor talking to your mum. Don't you?'

'Fu—sorry. I mean, I didn't know Amy was listening.'

'I was pretty shocked when she told me.'

'Are you going to tell Dad?'

'What do you think?'

When he didn't reply, she said, 'Blaine?'

'Huh?'

'Tell me about your conversations with Jason.'

'I shouldn't have listened to him.'

'Is that why you went home to your mum?'

'Everything was getting out of control and then I got scared when you saw the photo. I'd deleted it from my phone but I'd forgotten it would have downloaded automatically to the iPad.'

'Why did you delete it?'

'I didn't want to have anything more to do with Jason.'

'Jason gave you the photo?'

'Yes.'

'Did Jason tell you to hide my stuff?'

'Yes.'

'When did he say that?'

'The afternoon he spent in the house.'

'What did he say?'

'He said he had no dad when he was my age but he would have been furious if his mum had taken up with another man. He asked if it bothered me that you and Dad were together. I said I hated it and now Dad wanted to marry you and if you said yes, Dad and I would never go on holidays again.'

So, Jason had known that Conor planned to marry her. Aoife felt her stomach lurch.

'What did Jason say?'

'He said you didn't really love my dad. You were just bored and wanted something new to amuse you. He said he loved you and Amy, that you were a family and you belonged together.'

What the hell was the matter with Jason?

'Go on.'

'He said Dad wouldn't believe that because he loved you. He said my dad would be very hurt when you dumped him, but the sooner you broke up the easier it would be for him. Jason asked if I wanted you to break up.'

'And you said yes?'

'Uh-huh, and Jason said he'd help me. He said you would be mad if your stuff went missing and Dad would be mad if you blamed me.'

'Did he tell you to do anything else?'

'I was supposed to say that Mum and Dad were always on the phone and laughing together and that it made my step-dad mad.'

'But you didn't say that.'

'I couldn't. I wasn't talking to you.'

'What else did Jason tell you to do?'

'I was supposed to leave the photo of Lisa somewhere you'd find it.'

'You knew Lisa was dead, right?'

'Yes. Jason said if we used a dead person, you would never be able to find out it wasn't true.'

'When were you going to leave the photo for me to find?'

'I was supposed to do it before Mum arrived, but when Jason heard she was coming to Dublin he said to wait until she went home.'

'Why did he want you to wait?'

'I was supposed to tell you that Mum and Dad shared a bed while she was here. Jason said you would be so mad you wouldn't believe anything Dad said about the photo.'

'But you didn't say that.'

'I didn't get a chance. You weren't in the house when we got back from the airport and then that man attacked you.'

'You didn't want to upset me when I was hurt?'

'No. Well, yes, but that wasn't why. When that man attacked you, Jason ran away and left you. Dad would never have done that. Even Amy tried to help. When I realised Jason didn't love you, I knew he lied to me, so I deleted the photo from my phone. If I had remembered to delete it from the iPad, nobody would ever have known.'

'Where did Jason get the photo of you and Conor on the beach?'

'I sent it to him.'

'And the photo of Lisa?'

'It was on her Facebook page.'

'Lisa was on Facebook? I searched under her name and didn't find anything. What's her profile?'

'I don't know. Jason didn't tell me. He said he had someone hack into the account and then delete it. He didn't want anyone guessing where the photo came from.'

'How often did you and Jason meet?'

'Most times Dad and I came to your house. Amy would tell him we would be there and he'd always show up.'

'I love your dad, Blaine.'

'I know. I'm sorry.'

'It's not your fault. I used to believe everything Jason said, and I was a few years older than you at the time. If Jason talks to you again, Blaine, tell me. If you don't want to tell me, tell your mum or Conor.'

'I'm never speaking to him again, Aoife.'

'Oh my God! Aoife! What are you going to do?'

'Nothing.'

'Are you crazy? You have to do something?'

'Like what?'

'Tell him he's a complete bastard. Say he's never to

come near your house again and if you even see him in the distance, you're calling the police.'

'What good would that do, Orla? He's Amy's father. I can't keep him away from her.'

'She'd be far better off without him.'

'If he wasn't her father, certainly. I'd never let her any-where near him, but he is her dad and she loves him.'

'Only because she has no idea what he's really like.'

'And I hope she never finds out, because however much any of us dislike the fact, Jason is Amy's father and nothing can ever change that.'

'You're not going to say anything at all?'

'Not one word.'

'Well, at least you know Conor wasn't two-timing you.'

'I never really believed he was, but I was beginning to doubt myself.'

'He's not in the clear yet, Aoife. The phone list was still deleted off your computer.'

'That was the murderer. Not Conor.'

'There's also the fact that Lisa phoned Conor. Hours later she was dead.'

Aoife quickly forgot Orla's warning. She was more con-vinced than ever that Conor was the man she had always believed him to be. So what if Lisa had phoned him? Yes-terday it had seemed like Conor had been in a relationship with Lisa, but that had been a lie. There would be a reason-able explanation for the phone call also. Although it was strange Conor still hadn't been in touch. Even if he was preoccupied with work, shouldn't he have phoned her by now? Amy was demanding to know when she would see him again, and Aoife had no idea what to tell her.

When she returned to her car, Aoife checked her phone again. Two missed calls from Conor. Damn! She mustn't have heard him over the traffic. She texted him. 'Sorry I missed you and I'm sorry we argued. I've sorted every-thing out with Blaine. You were right; he hadn't been in my house, although he admitted he hid my stuff. It wasn't his fault. Jason put him up to it. Ring me when you get a chance.'

FORTY-THREE

AOIFE WATCHED AMY sleep. What kind of a life was she going to have with Jason as a father? If he could manipulate a fifteen-year-old who didn't even know him, what would he do to a three-year-old who loved him? Her mind flashed to a news story of a twelve-year-old who had murdered her mother and stepfather because her dad had talked her into it. Okay, that was enough. Aoife got up and went in search of her laptop. She needed something to distract her. Normal twelve-year-olds didn't murder people. It was time to stop being so dramatic.

Aoife was rereading her interview notes when a thought struck her. No matter how bad things were between them, Conor was not the type of man to walk away without another word. Even if he wanted a permanent break up, he would sit down with Aoife and talk about it. If Blaine's involvement had remained a secret, could they have had that discussion without Aoife mentioning the doctored photo? Conor was a detective. It was in his nature to get to the bottom of things. He would have asked questions and it would all have come out. Wouldn't it? Jason must know that was at least a possibility. And, knowing Jason, she was certain he had a plan B. What other use could he make of the photo? Oh my God! Did Jason intend to leak the photo to the media? Was that his next step? Imagine what the tabloid press would make of it. Within days, the entire country would believe Conor was a murderer. And how could he convince anyone of Jason's deception without involving Blaine? Conor would never do that. Nothing could be proved, of course, but the damage to his career would be catastrophic. How could their relationship survive that? Aoife leaned back against the headboard and took deep breaths to calm herself. Was everybody in her life going to have to pay for the mistake she'd made in marrying Jason?

This was getting her nowhere. The only thing she needed to worry about right now was the fact that a cold-blooded murderer had come to her house to kill her and possibly Amy. All her energy needed to go into finding the murderer and keeping them safe. Everything else could wait.

Aoife took out a notebook and jotted down her conclusions. Keith had the strongest motive to kill the Grogans, and he fitted the profile of an out-of-control lunatic. Martin had the strongest motive to kill Ruth. Neither had any reason to kill Lisa, so the logical assumption was she had discovered something that made her a threat. And that something must be linked to Natasha. First thing tomorrow, Aoife would find Natasha and interview her.

⁓

Aoife was beginning to wonder what she would do without Instagram. Natasha's account was even more informative than Susan's. She posted three or four times a day, changed boyfriends almost as often as she changed hairstyles and spent a minimum of four nights a week clubbing. It was unlikely she was a morning person. Aoife decided to wait until lunch and then hang out around her house and see if she appeared.

An hour into her stake-out, Jenny phoned.

'What are you up to today?'

'Trying to get a young girl to talk to me.'

'That doesn't sound very exciting. I'm on my way to M&S. Feel like a coffee break when I get back?'

Aoife checked her watch. It was two-thirty. For all she knew Natasha was at work. She should have realised the best place to catch her was in a club at the beginning of the night, when she was drunk enough to be careless but not too drunk to make sense.

'Sounds like a plan. Three-thirty?'

'Great. I'll bring the éclairs.'

Aoife popped into Dunnes Stores and bought a cheap, black lycra minidress and a pair of extremely uncomfortable shoes. That and a bit of make-up should be enough to get her into any club.

She texted Maura, asking if she would mind keeping

Amy for the night, and drove to Jenny's. It was three-twenty when she got to Jenny's house. She checked her phone to see if Conor had been in touch. He hadn't. Maura hadn't texted her either. Damn, the message had a little red exclamation mark beside it. It had been rejected because she was out of credit. Why had she bought a pay-as-you-go phone? Looking through her history, Aoife realised she'd been picking up the hotel's Wi-Fi, which had allowed her to send messages and make calls, but none of the messages she'd sent outside the hotel had gone through. She dialled the automatic top-up number in the hope that it had finally been fixed. No such luck. There wasn't time to go through the whole rigmarole of topping up through the operator. Experience had taught her that it took nine minutes of computerised messages before she would get to speak to a human. She stuffed her phone in her pocket. Maybe Conor would phone her.

When the door opened, Aoife was surprised to find Derek on the other side.

'Hi, Derek.'

'Hi, Aoife. Come in. Jenny popped out to the shops, but she'll be back shortly. I'm just getting some papers together for work. I'll be with you in a minute.'

Aoife went into the sitting room and sat down. As usual, the girls' textbooks were spread over the low coffee table. She picked up *Active Maths 1* and turned it over.

Twenty-four euros! Good God! She'd have to set up a text-book savings account if that was the price of just one book.

Derek hurried into the room. 'I phoned Jenny. She got stuck in traffic but she'll be here in about fifteen minutes. Do you mind if I leave you here to wait on your own?' He pointed at his files. 'I have to get to work.'

'No, that's fine. Derek, have you interviewed Ruth's nanny?'

'Who?'

'Ruth's nanny, Natasha.'

'I didn't, but I'm sure somebody in the department spoke to her. Why?'

'She was one of the last people Lisa spoke to, and I got the impression from Lisa's email that she believed what Natasha told her was significant.'

'What email?'

'Lisa was checking out the people Ruth spoke to in her last few weeks.'

Derek stiffened. 'And how would either you or Lisa get your hands on that information?'

Hell!

As she scrambled for a convincing answer, Aoife saw Derek's face darken. It was the exact expression he'd shown her the day he'd said she wasn't a suitable wife for Conor. His lips barely moved as he said, 'That is confidential information, Aoife.'

'Derek, I think it is a huge mistake for us to discuss the investigation. It never ends well. Let's forget I ever mentioned the subject.'

'Let's not. I'd like to know how you got your hands on information that has not been released to the public.'

'And I would like not to discuss it.'

'I don't think you understand what a serious matter this is.'

'Are you arresting me, Derek?'

After a short hesitation, Derek turned on his heel and left the room. He closed the door with such extraordinary gentleness, it was clear it was taking all his self-control not to bang it. A few minutes later he called. 'I'm leaving, Aoife. Please boil the kettle so Jenny doesn't have to wait when she comes home.'

Aoife sighed as she made her way to the kitchen. She had always admired Derek's devotion to Jenny, but this was ridiculous. Jenny wouldn't mind waiting a few minutes for the kettle to boil.

The kitchen table was set with two mugs, a packet of biscuits and two plates. Aoife's stomach gurgled at the sight of the biscuits. She hadn't eaten since breakfast and only now realised she was starving. Aoife had taken three steps towards the kettle when rough hands grabbed her. One hand covered her mouth; the other held a knife which was pointed at her throat.

'It didn't have to be like this, Aoife. I deleted that email so you'd never know Natasha existed. This is what comes of breaking the law. Now you've read the email, you've given me no choice.'

'Wh—?'

'I'm sorry, Aoife, but it's you or me.'

❧

'Aah!' Aoife gave a strangled reply.

'Hush. We have to get out of here before Jenny comes home. Move!' He pushed her towards the door that led from the kitchen to the garage.

Aoife tried to scream 'No!' but it came out as a muffled groan.

At that exact moment, a door banged and Jenny called, 'Sorry I'm late, Aoife, but I got the éclairs.'

There was a wide smile on her face as she sailed through the kitchen door carrying two M&S bags.

'Oh my God! Derek! What's going on?'

'Nothing to worry about, darling. Leave this to me.'

Aoife struggled. 'Jmm.'

'Why are you doing that to Aoife? Are you arresting her? What did she do?'

'I'm not arresting her, darling. I'm going to kill her.'

FORTY-FOUR

JENNY'S BAGS LANDED on the tiled floor with a clatter.

'You're going to—' She put a hand to her head. 'Der—Derek, if Aoife broke the law you have to arrest her. You can't take the law into your own hands. That would mean you were no better than a criminal.'

'Aoife didn't break the law, darling. I did. The only way I can avoid prison is to kill her.'

'You broke—Derek, what are you talking about?'

'It would take too long to explain now, darling. I'll tell you all about it tonight.' He tightened his grip on Aoife's mouth and pushed her towards the door.

'Nnnn!' Aoife tried to scream. She remembered her self-defence class and jammed her heel into his foot. Derek loosened his grip and she pulled away and raced past a startled Jenny to the front door.

Her hand was on the latch when Derek grabbed her. He covered her mouth with both hands. She managed to grab a tiny bit of flesh between her teeth and bit down. Derek grunted and attempted to shake his hand free, but Aoife held on for dear life. He lifted her off the floor and carried her into the kitchen. The door banged Jenny in the back but she didn't seem to notice. She was standing in the same spot, both hands covering her mouth.

Derek removed one hand from Aoife's mouth and hit her across the face. Aoife's head jerked to one side and Derek pulled his hand free. It took her a second to react, then Aoife took a deep breath and screamed, 'Help!'

Jenny jumped. Derek pulled the silk scarf from his wife's throat and stuffed it into Aoife's mouth. There was a tea towel drying on the radiator, and he grabbed it and tied it around her head. Then he dragged her to the corner, removed a set of handcuffs from his pocket and tied her to the radiator.

Leaving her completely helpless, head still ringing, Derek took Jenny by the hand and led her to a chair.

'I know it's a shock, darling, but everything's going to be okay. Now, I'm going to make you a cup of tea.' He picked up the bags of shopping she had dropped, removed the éclairs and placed a slightly battered one on her plate. 'You have a nice cake, and when I get back, I'll tell you all about it.'

'Nnn!' Aoife shook the handcuffs and banged her feet on the floor.

'Shut up, Aoife. That's not going to do a bit of good. Be grateful it's just you that's going to die. If I'd had to come to your house, I might have had to kill your daughter too.

Mind you, I don't want to kill you. You're annoying and have no respect for the law, but you don't deserve to die. Still, I always figured that if you left me with no choice, at least I'd have the pleasure of butchering Golden Boy Moloney too. Now that is something I would have enjoyed.'

He was pouring water into Jenny's cup when she grabbed his hand.

'Derek, what's going on?' Her voice was low and timid, very different from the confident, cheerful tone Aoife was accustomed to.

'Later, darling.'

'No, Derek. Now.' She was beginning to sound more like herself.

'There isn't time, my love.'

Jenny pushed back her chair. 'Derek Lehane, you tell me what is going on right now or I'm calling the police.'

Derek grabbed Jenny's bag, took out her phone and removed the battery.

'Darling, you can't phone the police. Do you want to see me arrested?'

'Arrested for what?' Jenny screamed.

'Hush, darling! There's no time to go into this. I can't kill Aoife here. It would leave too much evidence. I need to drive her to the house where I killed Lisa and dump her in the same alley. When I get back, we can have a long talk.'

'Where you killed Lis—I don't believe I'm hearing this.'

'Hush, my love. You don't need to worry about any

of this. None of it is your fault. I know you would never cheat on me.'

'I would never—Derek, one of us is going off their rocker and I think it might be me. Am I imagining this whole conversation? Did you really just tell me that you killed Lisa and you're going to kill Aoife because I would never cheat on you?'

'No, darling. It's complicated, but there's a girl called Natasha who had a recording that could send me to prison for life. I destroyed the recording, of course, but Natasha knows it existed. Lisa discovered this also. I killed Lisa, but I haven't had time to kill Natasha and there may be other recordings I don't know about yet. A few moments ago, Aoife told me she was planning to speak to Natasha. I can't let that happen. So, you see, they both need to die or I could go to prison for murdering Ruth.'

'Ruth—oh dear Lord. You killed Ruth? No, you couldn't have. The police would have found your DNA there.'

'They did. But I told them I'd called to her house to interview her. They expected to find my DNA, just as they expected to find it in Grogan's house. After all, the entire book club saw me call there the night of the party.'

'But why would you kill Ruth?'

'That was her fault.' He jerked his thumb at Aoife. 'When she told me what Ruth had done to Grogan's wife, I was so furious it took all my strength not to go to her house and tear her limb from limb that very minute.'

'For the love of God, Derek. Why?'

'Ruth tried to do to Grogan's wife what Grogan tried to do to me.'

'What are you talking about?'

'Grogan tried to steal you from me.'

⚭

'You think Shane and I—dear God, Derek, the thought never even crossed my mind.'

'I know it didn't, darling. But it crossed Shane's.'

Jenny shook her head 'No. No. No!'

'It did, my love. You're so good you never see the evil in others. When I came to collect you from Fiona's party, he put his arms around you right in front of me.'

'He hugged us all, Derek. It meant nothing.'

'And I saw the photo.'

'What photo?'

'The photo of him leaning over you at the birthday party.'

'He was trying to fit into the shot. That's all.'

'No, darling. That wasn't all. I saw the text he sent you too.'

'Shane never sent me any text.'

'Yes, he did. It said "like must marry like or there can be no happiness." He was telling you not to waste your time on an old fuddy-duddy like me. That bastard wanted you to believe you belonged with somebody like him. Someone young, good looking, the centre of attention at every party. Not stuck in a corner with me, with everybody trying to avoid us.'

Jenny groaned. 'It was a book, Derek. It was a quote from a book. Shane had no interest in me and I had no interest in him.'

'It was all part of a plan, darling. That bastard wanted you and he was determined to steal you from me.'

'I would never—'

'I know you wouldn't, darling. But he would have kept at it until you began to see me the way he did. Some dour—'

'No. I wouldn't—'

Derek kissed her. 'You would have kept your vows. You would have stuck by me to the bitter end. But you see, darling, I didn't want a bitter end for us. I wanted us to be happy.'

'We were happy!' Jenny wailed.

'We wouldn't have been for long. Not if I hadn't put an end to that bastard's plans.'

Jenny grabbed his hand. 'Derek, please tell me you didn't kill those babies.'

Derek nodded. 'Yes, my love, I did. Right in front of him. I showed him exactly what it felt like to lose your family.'

FORTY-FIVE

JENNY WAS SITTING at the kitchen table, head down on her arms, sobbing. Derek patted her head, muttering, 'Hush, darling. It will be okay.'

Jenny's head jerked up. 'Don't touch me!'

'Okay, my love. It's the shock. You'll see I did what I had to do to protect our family.'

'You are completely insane.'

Derek laughed. 'No, my darling. I've never been saner.'

'You think you're sane? Even if you hated Shane, what did Fiona and the kids ever do to you?'

'You're missing the point, darling. I needed to see Grogan's face when he realised he had lost his family. Besides, they had more than one chance to fight back but I was too clever for them. Fiona came out of her bedroom as I was climbing in the bathroom window. If she had reacted faster, the outcome would have been very different. Instead, I put the knife to her throat and forced her to walk into the kitchen. Grogan was on his phone. He jumped up when he saw her. Before he could say one word, I cut her throat right in front of him.'

'Don't tell me anymore. I don't want to know.'

'The point I'm trying to make is that they had the opportunity to fight back. Shane could have charged at me. Instead, he ran over to Fiona, pulled her into his arms and started screaming. How stupid was that?'

'Shut up!'

'Darling! What's come over you? Don't speak like that.'

'Go to hell, Derek.'

'You don't mean that. You're upset about the kids. They got in the way and they were part of my revenge.'

When Jenny didn't reply he said 'In retrospect, maybe I should have let the youngest live. I promised Grogan that I would. It was the only way to get him to sign the suicide note and cut his own wrists. Honestly, Jenny, I intended to keep my word but who knows how much a child that age would remember as she grew older? I couldn't take the risk.'

Aoife hadn't realised she was crying until the tears landed on her jeans. She looked at Jenny, who was sitting with her hands covering her face. Nobody spoke. Nobody moved. It was like they were all stuck in a bubble where images of the scenes Derek had described were played over and over. After what felt like an age, Jenny pushed back her chair and stood up. She held her arms out to Derek.

'Oh my darling. I knew you'd understand.'

Jenny shook her head. 'I don't understand, Derek. But you're my husband and I swore to love and take care of you.' She pulled away. 'Now, if we're going to do this, let's do it properly. Where's your gun?'

FORTY-SIX

'WE CAN'T SHOOT her, Jenny. I don't have a silencer. The neighbours would phone the police.'

'Couldn't we use a cushion? I've seen that in the movies.'

Aoife banged her feet against the radiator.

Jenny didn't even glance in her direction. 'Shut up, Aoife, or I'll cut your throat myself. Derek, if we're going to move Aoife to another location, we need a gun. You can only kill one person at a time with a knife.'

'I wasn't planning on killing anyone else—well, other than that Natasha whore, and that's proving a real challenge. She's yet to spend two consecutive nights in her own bed.'

'You weren't planning to kill Ruth or Lisa either, were you? These things happen. Now, you get your gun, I'll find a blanket to wrap the body in and we can get out of here.'

They joined hands as they left the room. Aoife pulled at the handcuffs. Jenny was just as insane as her husband.

How the hell was she going to get out of here? She took a few deep breaths and tried to calm herself. Her chance would come. Lisa had been killed on the north side. If Derek planned to murder her in the same location, he would have to drive her across the city. She would keep her wits about her and wait for her opportunity. The important thing was not to panic.

Derek came back to the kitchen, threw his shoulder holster on the table and stuck the gun in his pocket. A few seconds later, Jenny joined him.

'Are you ready, darling?'

'Give me one second.' Jenny sat down and pushed her head between her knees.

Derek rushed over to her.

'What's wrong?'

'I don't feel great.'

'Did you take your blood pressure medicine this morning?'

Jenny shook her head.

'I'll be back in a minute.'

As soon as he left the room, Aoife tapped on the radiator.

'Jnn.'

Jenny jumped up, grabbed the holster and pulled at something. Oh my God, it was a key!

FORTY-SEVEN

JENNY RACED OVER to Aoife. Unlocked the handcuffs and untied the tea towel from around her head. Aoife spat out the scarf.

'Quick, Aoife. We have to get out of here before he comes back.'

She helped Aoife to stand and half pulled her towards the kitchen door. They were almost there when the kitchen door opened.

'Jenny, what are you doing?' Derek removed the gun from his pocket and pointed it at Aoife's head.

❦

Jenny stood in front of Aoife.

'I'm helping you, Derek. Things are bad, but we can fix them. You, I and Aoife are going to drive to the airport. We'll empty our bank accounts and you will get on the first plane out of the country. I'll keep Aoife with me for three days. Then I'll let her go. You will be free and nobody else has to die.'

'No, Jenny. I would die without you and the girls.'

'We'll buy phones nobody can trace and you'll phone me when you're settled. The girls and I will join you wherever you are.'

'It's too risk—what the hell is she doing?'

Aoife had taken her phone out of her pocket. As Jenny swung around, she hit 'send' on the text message. Derek raced across the room and knocked the phone from her hand. The screen cracked as it landed on the tiled floor. He picked it up and said, 'Bloody Moloney. She told the bastard I was the murderer.'

Grabbing his own phone, he pressed a number. 'Hi, Alan. Is the DI in?…No, that's okay. I've been delayed myself. Don't say anything. I might make it before he does. Talk to you later.'

He put the phone back in his pocket and, keeping the gun pointed at Aoife's head, used his other hand to wipe the sweat from his forehead.

'It's over, Jenny. There's nothing else I can do. Moloney will be here in no time.'

'You can use me as a hostage,' Aoife said. 'Carry out Jenny's plan, only make the police take you to the airport. Jenny can keep me here until you're safe.'

Derek grabbed her and held the knife to her throat.

'Do you think I'm an idiot, Aoife? I would never make it to the airport.'

'Yes, you would.' Aoife barely opened her mouth, careful not to jerk the knife. 'Conor is a man of his word.'

'Oh, will you shut up. I am so sick of hearing about the great Detective Inspector Moloney. I do most of the work in that department and he sits at his desk taking all the credit. That should have been my job. How do you think it feels reporting to a jumped-up nobody like him?'

Keeping her voice low and calm, Aoife said, 'Whatever you think of Conor, he loves me. He wouldn't do anything to endanger me.'

'She's right, darling. We can still work this out.'

'No, Jenny, we—'

They all froze as a door banged shut and Caoimhe shouted, 'Hi, Mum. What's for dinner?'

Jenny yelled, 'Go do your homework! We're having dinner in the sitting room.'

The kitchen door swung open 'But I'm star—Dad, Mum, what's going on?'

Jenny rushed over and put an arm around her daughter.

'Your dad is arresting Aoife. It's a long story and I'll tell you about it later. Where's your sister?'

'She stopped at Nessa's. I told her not to be late for dinner.'

Jenny took her wallet from her bag and held it out. 'I haven't had time to make dinner. Go around to Nessa's, get your sister and take a taxi into town. Go someplace nice for dinner and then go to the movies. By the time you get home, your Dad and I will have all this sorted.'

'But—'

'No time for buts, Caoimhe. Go now.'

'Jenny, I don't think that's a good idea.'

'What are you talking about?'

'I can't fix this, Jenny. It's the end of the road for us.'

'Mum, what—'

'Derek, let Caoimhe take care of her sister and we'll work this out when she's gone.'

'No.' He held out his arm. 'Come here, Caoimhe.'

'No!' Jenny grabbed her daughter's hand and pushed her towards the door. 'Get out now!'

'What's happening? Mum! Dad!'

'Caoimhe, I need your help.'

Caoimhe moved closer as Jenny shouted, 'No!'

'Good girl,' Derek said. He threw the knife on the floor and covered it with his foot. Keeping one arm around Aoife's neck, he put the other around Caoimhe's shoulder.

Aoife struggled, but he tightened his grip until she was having difficulty breathing.

'Sit down, Jenny.'

Jenny didn't move. Both hands covered her mouth.

'Dad?'

'It's okay, Caoimhe. I'm going to take care of everything. Now, Jenny, your plan about the airport is never going to work. There is only one option left.'

'What?'

'When we married, I swore to take care of you until

the day I died. I promised you that I would always be there for the girls. You know I always keep my word. I can't be there for our family the way I would like to be. Aoife and her text have seen to that. But we can all still be together.'

'You don't mean—'

'It's the only way, darling.'

FORTY-EIGHT

'NO, NO, DEREK. Not the girls. You can take me with you, but the girls stay here.'

'We can't leave them on their own. What kind of parents would that make us?'

'Dad, where are you going?'

'Hush, Caoimhe. This is important. I have to make your mother understand.'

'Understand what?'

'Caoimhe! I told you to be quiet! Jenny, I need your help. If I have to go, bloody Golden Boy Moloney isn't getting to have his family either.' He waved his fingers in the air. 'I'm kind of tied up here. You're going to have to take care of Aoife.'

'Dad!'

Caoimhe tried to pull away from her father. As he went to grab her, Aoife took the opportunity to sink her teeth into his arm. Derek yelped. She kicked him in the shin and raced for the front door.

Derek picked up the knife and pointed it at Caoimhe's throat. 'Stop her, Jenny, or I'll do it right now.'

Jenny screamed, 'No!' She raced after Aoife, flung herself on top of her and knocked her to the floor. Derek joined them, knife still to Caoimhe's throat. He kicked Aoife in the stomach.

'Dad!'

'Caoimhe, hush! You mum's going to take care of Aoife. Then all three of us will sit down and wait for your sister. I'll explain it all to you then.'

'Derek!'

'Jenny, take the gun out of my pocket and shoot Aoife.'

'Dad, no! Please!'

Derek shouted over Caoimhe's sobs. 'Jenny, do it now or Caoimhe will have to go first.'

Jenny's hand shook as she removed the gun from Derek's pocket.

'You know how to fire it. Do it.'

'Let Caoimhe go. Then I'll kill Aoife.'

'No, my love. You're a good mother. It's only right that you would put your daughter before me, but I can't have you shooting me before I've done my duty by all of you.'

'I can't shoot her while she's that close to Caoimhe. What if I miss?'

Derek sighed.

'That box you were going to give to charity, the one with the girls' old toys. Where is it?'

'In the garage.'

'Get it.'

'What?'

'Hurry!'

'Dad, please!'

'Caoimhe, listen to me. You're too young to under-stand, so you'll have to take my word that I'm doing what's best for my family. I can't have you ruining it, so if you make one more sound, your sister dies the second she sets foot inside this house. Tell me you understand.'

'Yes,' Caoimhe sobbed as Jenny ran back into the room carrying a large box.

'Take out the skipping ropes.'

'Why?'

'Because it's important. Bring them over here. Now tie one end of the rope to Aoife's hand.' He wiggled the knife at Caoimhe's throat. 'Remember, I'll use this if I have to.'

Jenny tied the knot.

'Hold it up so I can see it.'

Derek examined it and shook his head.

'No. That's not good enough. Double-knot it and pull it tighter. Use her right hand.'

'Aoife's left-handed,' Jenny lied.

'Okay, her left hand, then.'

Jenny held up the knot for inspection.

'Good. Now give me one end of the rope and move Aoife as far away from me as possible.'

Jenny took Aoife's arm and led her about three feet

away. Derek yanked at the rope. 'That's good. Now, use the second rope to tie her to the kitchen chair.'

'Not there,' Derek said as Jenny placed the rope around Aoife's waist. 'Tie it above her chest. Make sure her arms are by her side.'

The rope was so loose, Aoife could already move one hand. A bit of wiggling and it would be free.

'Now you have enough space, darling. Shoot her.'

'I can't! Oh God, Derek! Stop this madness.'

Caoimhe yelped as Derek dug the tip of the knife into her throat.

'Stop! Stop! I'll do it.' Jenny held the gun in the air and pointed it at Aoife's head. 'I'm sorry, Aoife. I'm so sorry.'

Aoife struggled with the rope. It loosened but didn't give. She rocked the chair from side to side, put all her weight against the back and knocked the chair over.

The gun went off.

Aoife was on the floor, still pulling at the ropes, when Derek said, 'Didn't I teach you better than that, Jenny? Anyone could have made that shot. You were nowhere near her.'

'She moved.'

'What did you expect? You should have aimed at her stomach. You could have shot her in the head later.'

Aoife yanked at the ropes as Caoimhe cried.

'It's not my fault, Derek. I tried.'

'You didn't try very hard, darling. Golden Boy mustn't

have checked his phone yet, but the neighbours will have heard the shot and called the police. You're wasting the little time we have left, and it's precious time the three of us could be spending together. We deserve a last few moments as a happy family. Don't ruin it.'

'I'm doing my best.'

'No, you're not, Jenny. Now, walk over to Aoife and put the gun against her head.'

'What?'

'You heard me. Put the gun against her head. And remember, if you do anything stupid, Caoimhe won't get to enjoy any family time.'

'I can't do it, Derek. I just can't.'

'You have until the count of ten. Nine...eight... seven...six...five...'

'Okay, okay, stop.'

'Four...three...'

Jenny raced over to Aoife and held the gun to her temple.

'Two...'

Jenny shut her eyes. Caoimhe screamed as the gun fired.

FORTY-NINE

AOIFE HAD FINALLY managed to free one arm. She used her shoulder to knock the gun out of Jenny's hand. As the gun crashed to the floor, Aoife pulled the rope over her head. She yanked at the second rope, but the knot wouldn't give. She was still tied to Derek.

Keeping one arm around Caoimhe's neck, Derek pulled at his end. Even with one hand, he was stronger than she was. Aoife hooked one foot around the leg of the kitchen table. Good! He'd have to let go of Caoimhe to use both hands. Pulling Caoimhe into a standing position, Derek pushed her in Aoife's direction. Jenny got to her feet.

'Jenny, pick up the gun, hold it to her head and shoot her.'

Jenny didn't reply.

'We'll start again. Ten…nine…eight…'

Jenny walked to the gun. As she bent to pick it up, Aoife unwound her foot from the kitchen table. Taking advantage of the extra length she had gained when Derek moved closer, Aoife reached out her foot and kicked the gun away. It landed a couple of inches from her hand. She stretched out her hand as Derek yanked on the rope. Without the table to latch on to, Aoife slid across the floor. She pointed the gun at Derek's head.

⤺

'Drop the rope.'

Derek did as she instructed but he kept the knife to Caoimhe's throat.

'Take that gun from her, Jenny. Do it now.'

'Derek—'

'Remember, I always keep my prom—Caoimhe! Stop that! I told you what would happen to your sister if you made a fuss. Jenny, this needs to be over right now. Take that gun from her.'

Aoife was now sitting on the floor. As Jenny moved closer, she raised the gun, pointed it at Derek's head and fired.

⤺

Caoimhe and Jenny screamed. Derek fell to the floor and all three stood frozen, looking down at him.

Caoimhe ran to her mother. Jenny put her arms around her and looked over her head at Aoife.

'I would have shot you.'

'I know.'

They heard the sirens in the distance. Aoife motioned towards Derek.

'Are you okay?'

Jenny nodded. She hugged Caoimhe tighter. 'Whoever that lunatic was, he wasn't my husband.'

FIFTY

Two days later...

IT HAD NEVER occurred to Aoife that she would be arrested. In her entire life, she had never expected to be brought to a police station against her will, to be finger-printed and cautioned. Three hours later she had been released on condition that she return for questioning at 8 a.m. the following morning. She was expecting it to be difficult. She had no idea how difficult. The very fact that every word she said was being taped was intimidating in itself. They allowed her three short breaks, but the inter-views went on forever. Conor had warned her she would be there all day. He was right. At ten minutes to midnight, they told her she was free to leave.

As promised, Conor was waiting to take her home.

'That's it, Aoife. They won't bother you again.'

'Are you sure?'

'Positive.'

'I'm so tired.'

'Stay in my house tonight. I'll get us a takeaway.'

'No. I want to see Amy.'

Conor drove her to Kildare. Aoife was too exhausted to talk, but she couldn't sleep either. Conor turned on the radio and switched it to Lyric FM. Neither of them liked the channel much, but it seemed appropriate for her mood.

After a half hour, she began to feel more like herself.

'Have you ever killed anybody, Conor?'

'No.'

'I didn't expect it to feel like this.'

'What do you feel?'

'Nothing.'

'You're probably in shock, Aoife. It might take a few days before it hits you.'

'What if I never feel anything?'

'It wouldn't bother me. Would it bother you?'

'I don't know. Could I be the same person if I can kill another human and not care?'

'You killed a monster who butchered children.' Conor shook his head. 'I still can't believe it. Derek Lehane! I thought he was the most moral person I had ever met. How could I not have seen who he really was? For God's sake, I'm supposed to be a detective.'

'Derek kept himself to himself. Everybody avoided him

in social situations. You told me you never spoke to him about anything but work.'

'And why didn't it occur to me that I should be concerned about that?'

'Don't blame yourself, Conor. We all thought Derek was the quiet, calm type. None of us could have guessed that beneath was a pot of simmering rage. It must have been bubbling away for years. Your promotion and the fear that Shane was trying to steal his family blew the lid off.'

'I'm not surprised he resented my promotion, but I never guessed the depth of his hatred.'

'None of us did, not even Jenny. Although I thought it was strange that he always referred to you as "Detective Inspector". Who else calls you by your full title?'

'Nobody. But Derek was always so formal, it seemed to fit with his personality.'

'I think the formality was a shield. It kept people at a distance so it was easier for him to hide his real feelings. Every time he said "Detective Inspector", I think he meant it as sarcasm. Almost like saying "here comes the so-called Detective Inspector. Isn't he pathetic" kind of thing.'

'He wasn't wrong. I was pathetic. My right-hand man was murdering all around me and I thought he was a decent, honourable man who respected the law.'

'I think the law was an outlet for Derek's anger. It gave him power, something he obviously needed desperately. He got to watch people at their lowest and feel satisfaction in his own part in bringing them down.'

'How did Jenny not see that something was wrong?'

'It's possible his relationship with Jenny was what motivated him to keep his anger under control. She and the kids were the one good thing in his life. They were the only people who enjoyed his company. To an extent, I believe he tried to live up to Jenny's idea of him. When I asked him why he became a policeman, he said it was to protect families. Through his family's eyes, Derek saw an ideal version of himself. Maybe that's why he told Jenny about the cases he was assigned. He was casting himself in the role of the hero. And that's the way his family saw him, so to Derek, families were sacrosanct. Anybody who threatened his family or, to a lesser extent, any family, deserved to die.'

'And Jenny?'

'Jenny saw what she wanted to see. She said that when she first knew him, Derek barely spoke to her. She filled his silences with what she wanted to believe he was thinking. And when something seemed off, it was easily explained by the stress of his job. When she phoned me to tell me that Ruth was murdered, she mentioned that she had known something was wrong with Derek the previous evening. When she asked him about it, he said he was upset about work. Like they say, "there are none so blind…"'

'I saw Jenny today. She was in the reception area as I walked by.'

'Did you speak to her?'

'I probably should have, but I couldn't. She tried to kill you.'

'Maybe I would have killed her if somebody was threatening Amy.'

'I understand why she did it, Aoife. I just can't forgive her.'

'Yeah, I'm having a bit of difficulty with that too.'

'You have to promise me one thing.'

'What?'

'The next time you decide to leave your home for three days, at least text me. That entire day I was camped outside your house waiting for you. If you had managed to send that text, what could I have done from Kildare?'

'That reminds me, I still haven't topped up that stupid phone.'

'Well, put money in it before the weekend. I don't want to be in England worrying that I can't contact you.'

'I will. Tell Blaine he's welcome in my house any time and make sure he understands that I don't blame him for anything. Jason is a master manipulator. Most adults can't see through him. No teenager could be expected to.'

FIFTY-ONE

Three weeks later…

AOIFE WAS SHOCKED at how quickly life returned
to normal.

When Conor wasn't working, he was in Aoife's house.
The one thing that had changed was he never mentioned
getting engaged any longer. She had been through an
incredibly traumatic time, he said. She needed a completely
stress-free life. Now wasn't the time to make life-chang-
ing decisions.

Summer was coming to an end and they were taking
advantage of every minute of the good weather. Each evening they went for a long walk. Amy spent the first half of
the walk trying to race them on her tricycle and the second
half riding on Conor's shoulders.

'Horsie, horsie!'

'Enough horsie, Amy. I need a rest.'

'But I want to play horsie!'

'We'll play again tomorrow. Would you like to know a secret, Amy?'

'Yes, please.'

'You're going to get to see Blaine tomorrow.'

'Blainey! When?'

'When you get back from kindergarten.'

'Blaine's coming for the weekend?' Aoife asked.

Conor put a finger to his lips. 'It's a secret between Amy and me. You'll have to wait to see what happens.'

The next day when Aoife collected Amy from kindergarten, she raced into the house, shouting, 'Blainey! Blainey!'

Conor called, 'In the kitchen.'

Aoife followed her into the kitchen. In the centre of the table, Conor had set up his laptop. He turned the screen around and there was Blaine.

'Blainey! You're Zooming!'

Aoife laughed.

She turned to Conor, but he had left the room. She found him standing in the hall, staring out the peephole in the front door.

'What are you doing out here?'

'Keeping watch.'

'For what?'

'That's it. I knew he'd come. Make sure Amy doesn't leave the kitchen, Aoife.'

'What?'

Conor didn't reply. He opened the front door and strode outside.

Aoife checked on Amy. Blaine was encouraging her to sing some song she'd learned in kindergarten.

Aoife closed the kitchen door and followed Conor outside. He was crossing the road towards a man who was half-hidden by a chestnut tree. As Conor approached, the man moved out of the shadows.

It was Jason.

'Oh God!' Aoife ran towards them.

'Don't come any closer, Aoife,' Conor shouted when she reached the edge of the footpath. 'This won't take long.'

He turned to Jason. 'I'm guessing Amy told you Blaine would be here today.'

'I don't know what you're talking about, Conor. I'm here to see my daughter.'

'Jason, I have no intention of arguing with you. I just want to make sure you understand me. When Aoife was attacked and you ran away like a pathetic coward, I wondered what kind of a toe-rag would do such a thing, but I said nothing. Your relationship with Aoife is none of my business. Your relationship with Amy is none of my business. Your relationship with my son is.'

Aoife gasped as Conor raised his fist and punched Jason in the nose.

'Do not ever speak to Blaine again.'

Jason howled. 'Ow! Jesus Christ! What the hell is wrong with you?'

He put his hands up to his nose. His eyes widened in horror when they came away covered in blood.

'You broke my nose. You actually broke my nose, you psycho!'

Conor walked away. 'No, I didn't.'

'This is assault,' Jason yelled after him. 'I'm calling the police.'

Conor didn't even turn around. 'I am the police, remember?'

'I'm reporting you to your superiors.'

'For what? I never laid a hand on you.'

'You broke my nose.'

'Your word against mine. I don't see any witnesses.'

'Aoife is a witness. You saw what he did, Aoife. Do you want to be married to a man who makes vicious unprovoked attacks on the father of your child?'

Aoife turned her back and walked away. As she closed the front door, Jason called, 'You'll be a battered wife next, Aoife. Or has he started beating you already?'

Conor came in behind her.

'I had to do it, Aoife.'

'You should have told me.'

'You'd have tried to stop me.'

'Yes, I would.'

'He screwed with my kid, Aoife. Jason needs to know that if he screws with the people I love, he will get hurt.'

'Are you going to beat up Keith too?'

VAL COLLINS

'What?'

'Keith did a lot more damage to your kid, Jason. He could have killed him.'

'The courts will take care of Keith, and this isn't about revenge, Aoife. It's about keeping us safe. Jason has proved he's scared of physical confrontation, so I wanted him to understand that if he messed with us, he would get hurt.'

'It's not that simple, Conor. I'm certain Jason is scared of you and I'm sure that from now on he'll avoid you as much as possible, but that won't stop him from trying to destroy us. You've just made things worse. And Amy's the one who will pay.'

EPILOGUE

Five weeks later…

CONOR CAME WITH her to the funeral. Aoife had been nervous about seeing Keith again, but he wasn't there. Presumably his dislike of Lisa extended to her mother.

'I'm so sorry,' Aoife said to Eamonn as the congregation lined up to offer their condolences to the immediate family.

'Thank you, Aoife. And thank you for giving her a little peace at the end. She's with Lisa and Shane now. That's all she ever wanted.'

⌘

'Thank God that's over. I know Lisa would have wanted me to be there, but I absolutely hate funerals.'

Conor pulled her into a hug. 'Somebody your age shouldn't have to know so much about them. Let's go into town. We need something to cheer ourselves up.'

As they walked down Grafton Street, Aoife pulled her jacket around her. Autumn had arrived. In many ways it was Aoife's favourite season. Once you gave up any hope of a heatwave and accepted you were heading for a bleak, miserable winter, every bright, sunny day seemed like a little miracle. Who cared about a bitter wind when the sky was clear and blue?

'Are you hungry, Conor?'

'Aren't I always?'

'Let's have lunch in Brown Thomas.'

They walked up the pedestrian street, arm in arm, stopping to listen to a busker. A large crowd had gathered in the centre of the road, singing along to Don McClean's 'American Pie.' Aoife and Conor joined in. Conor's arm was around her and his voice boomed out over the crowd. Aoife stopped singing to listen to him. Didn't Don McClean's wife claim her husband was very controlling? Aoife thought of Jenny, who had been so happily married to a monster. She thought of Jason and the disastrous mistake she had made in choosing him as Amy's father. She would never make such a stupid mistake again.

'Conor?'

He didn't hear her above the noise of the crowd. She looked around and saw the green shop awning to their right. He would be able to hear her there. Grabbing his arm, she led him towards it.

'What's wrong?' he asked.

She pointed at the jewellery shop window.

'I thought you might like to buy me a ring.'

Hi,

Thank you for choosing THE SILENT SPEAK. If you enjoyed it, it would be great if you could spare a moment to write a review. It doesn't have to be long, one line is perfect.

THE SILENT SPEAK is my third book. My first two books are GIRL TARGETED and ONLY LIES REMAIN. You can check them out here: http://bit.ly/2Xw7vTb

All my books are stand alone thrillers but GIRL TARGETED and ONLY LIES REMAIN cover earlier periods in Aoife's life.

If you would like to get in touch, the link above will take you to my website where you can send me a message, sign up for my newsletter and find all my social media links.

I'm always excited to hear from readers so please do get in touch.

Val

ACKNOWLEDGMENTS

Thank you to my editor, copy editor, and book designer. This is the third book that Debz Hobbs-Wyatt, Eliza from Clio Editing and Patrick Knowles have helped me produce. Their assistance is always invaluable and I don't know how I would manage without them.

I'd also like to thank Suzy Pope, my new editor, who proofread this book and offered many helpful suggestions.

If you're reading this book, it's thanks mostly to Liz Psaltis, my marketing guru. Without her nobody would know THE SILENT SPEAK even exists.

As always I would like to thank my friends:

Tina – always the first person outside my family to read my book and offer perfect advice.

John – A fount of knowledge on the workings of the Irish police force and the only reason I can mention the police in my books without making a complete idiot of myself.

Yvonne – Who always comes up with an idea whenever I run out of them.

Most of all, I'm grateful to my family – those who are still with me and those who are gone.

Made in the USA
Coppell, TX
01 September 2021